WEIGHT

By Dan Rempala

WEIGHT

CHAPTER ONE:
TREADING WATER

Rick Shaw's scarred and bloodied fingers wrapped themselves around the handle of his weapon as his weary feet stomped up the hill. He moved through the swaying grass like a Clydesdale, all kinetic power and forward lean. Other than the soft stomp of his deliberate gate, only the distant rumble of thunder broke the stillness. At the top of the hill, like a trio of vultures waiting for death's descent, stood three of General Something's elite guard. Rick stopped his advance with a little over ten yards to spare, enough of a distance to keep his opponents triangulated in his visual field, waiting to see what they would do. If they tried to rush him, he could use the incline and loss of elevation to his advantage; it was one of [his mentor's] first lessons: if he's stupid enough to let you, use your opponent's momentum against him.

As Rick discretely let his fingers flex around the handle of his weapon, his eyes darted from opponent to opponent, reading every movement and non-movement. The one on his left and the middle one breathed shallow breaths, waiting patiently for him to tip his hand, but the one on the right stood stiff as a board and sucked in a gutful of air right when Rick's eyes fell on him, identifying himself as the first to die.

Like clockwork, the enemy to Rick's right stepped forward, screaming, and discharged/swung his or her own weapon. With inches to spare, Rick sidestepped the attack, but before he could take advantage of his opponent's vulnerable position, what had started as a faint rumbling in the ground quickly turned into a crescendo. Everyone froze, even Rick, as the ground opened up and inhaled all three enemies, their weapons, and a couple tons of soft turf. If Rick hadn't thrown himself down the hill the instant that the first traces of dirt sprayed skyward, it might have taken him, too. He slammed his shoulder into the ground and rolled to one knee a couple yards away, in time for his eyes to register the new, distinctly larger combatant that entered the fray. Stepping off/out of the mighty beast/machine, this person's first move was to lift its helmet off of its head and let a row of blond(e) locks cascade over its shoulders.

Tension leaked out of Rick's shoulders at the sight of the familiar face and his lungs pulled in some of the clean, country air. Life gradually sped up as his brain shifted out of "combat mode." He climbed the rest of the way to his feet and allowed his weapon to return to its holster/scabbard. "You're a little late," Rick said, casually lifting an eyebrow. Relieved as he felt, it wouldn't do anyone any good for him to show weakness, to imply anything other than that he had everything sorted. "And you need a little more practice with that thing; another couple feet and you would have taken me with them."

"I hit the bull's eye," the blond(e) person assured him as the thing that (s)he arrived on/in made a characteristic noise, as if voicing agreement. "But I am sorry I'm late; I got held up at the location we visited earlier."

"No problem," Rick said, reflexively scanning the landscape. Partly, it was a habit he'd developed after years on the battlefield, searching for and cataloguing potential threats before letting his combat-readiness fall by another notch, but he mainly did it now as a show of self-reliance, as if ignoring help made it less necessary. Gratitude was hard for him these days. It had been years since the Battle of Something Bay, and he wasn't the sort who liked to look back, anyway, but betrayal

sticks to you like a cancer. "I had everything under control. The important thing is
that you're here now."

"Listen, Rick," the blond(e) person said, hesitantly, unable to meet his eyes.
"Um, what happened earlier… at that place where something dangerous happened and
I behaved un-heroically…"

Rick cut him/her off by slapping him/her on his/her strong/supple shoulder
in a gesture of camaraderie. No, gratitude didn't come naturally to him anymore, but
with effort, he could follow the appropriate social norms. "What's done is done," he
assured the other person, forcing himself to smile and make eye contact. He was
surprisingly tolerant of weakness, just not his own. "There's no point in dwelling on
the past, so all I have to say is, thank you, secondary character, for that thing you just
did."

*   *   *

"I don't mean to sound insensitive and all… because I can tell by
the way you're looking at me, you're proud of yourself," Shirley said as
she leaned to the edge of the balcony and blew a stream of smoke into the
air current rushing down Fourth Avenue, "but that's worse than shit."
The smoke stream dissolved within a second, but it lasted longer than her
good will had; it was her first cigarette of the workday, and Derrick was
ruining the taste.

"Only if you're strictly dwelling on the negatives," Derrick said,
standing several wary feet from the railing. She'd noticed this tendency
earlier, and he had explained his manifold reasons to keep his distance.
First, he was a self-diagnosed acrophobic, probably because the town
where he grew up didn't have any standing structure that exceeded two
stories, except for maybe a few grain silos and the water tower. He had
no love of for cigarette smoke, either, not because of phobias, but for
health and cosmetic reasons. Cigarettes gave the average adult nicotine-
addict the lung capacity of a hummingbird and the aroma of week-old

coffee grounds. Finally, he was a still little high from the oxycontin tablet he'd popped two hours earlier, and even though the label on the bottle didn't warn against standing next to ledges atop tall buildings, it should have. "Plus, first drafts are supposed to suck."

"I have to dwell on the negatives if that's all you give me," Shirley insisted, her free hand stuffed inside the corresponding pocket of her long, black, wool coat, "but there aren't even a lot of those. And I wouldn't even qualify this as a synopsis; a synopsis gives you a glimpse of the larger picture. This is like a half-chapter outline with complete sentences. All we know is that it's an adventure story, one with a character with light-colored hair—"

"I'm not married to either of those ideas," Derrick interjected, as if those were the roadblocks inhibiting her enjoyment of his masterpiece.

"—and the main characters name is 'Rick Shaw.'"

"Well, that part's pretty cool, right?" Derrick offered. "I thought of that, like, six months ago, when I was watching the second *Indiana Jones* movie, but I came up with the rest of it last week."

"It has its charms," she offered, generously, "but it isn't exactly a substitute for a decent plot."

"Fine, what about 'Man versus Society.'"

Shirley started to bring the cigarette to her lips, but paused long enough to ask, "As what?"

"As a plot."

"This isn't multiple-choice. You don't even know whether your protagonist is a wayward knight or a space ranger. These things matter." As she spoke, Shirley brandished the cigarette about like an orchestra conductor with a tiny, white baton. She was very aware of the habit, and it was a major reason she couldn't give up smoking; otherwise, she didn't know what to do with her hands. "I appreciate you trying to be more accessible with your writing, but this…" Shirley inhaled deeply "… this isn't you at all." Technically, tenants weren't supposed to smoke on the building grounds, even the balcony, but people cut you some slack when you're standing outside on the twenty-fourth floor; you're only spreading cancer to yourself and the pigeons. "And I could see how the secondary character could get *out* of a machine that tunneled through the ground, but how could it get *off* of something that did the same?"

"Like if the secondary character was riding a giant worm or a badger or something that burrowed," Derrick said, holding his hands out in front of him like a Tyrannosaurus Rex and making a digging motion with his hands. "Like if she put a saddle on it."

"She?"

He shrugged, admitting, "I'm leaning toward a she."

"That's physically impossible," Shirley told him, with all the authority of someone with a doctorate in Burrowing speaking to a layman. "If you put a saddle on a giant worm, then let it burrow through the ground, you'd get a face full of dirt, and you'd either fall off the saddle or you'd choke and you'd die."

"Great," Derrick said, matter-of-factly, his hands jammed in his pants pockets and his shoulders riding high and stiff. He wore blue jeans and an olive-drab army jacket, the kind of outfit one would not wear if anticipating a twenty-minute conversation on the twenty-fourth-floor balcony. Sometimes, during the wintery months, Shirley liked to bring non-smoking, underdressed people out to the ledge for conversations because she could throw on a nice, thick pea coat and assume an immediate negotiating advantage over the poor sap who just wanted to go back inside. More than once, she scheduled a meeting with a client or a publishing rep based on the weather forecast. "Problem solved: it's a science-fiction adventure and the secondary character was riding in a digging machine."

"That's not how you do it," Shirley groaned.

"That's not how *you* do it; I have my own methods," Derrick said. When Shirley bristled, he must have recognized the haughtiness in his tone because he quickly added, "Look, every great story has to have a great name for the main character: Jay Gatsby. Atticus Finch. Tinsy Norgay."

"Norgay was a real person," Shirley corrected, "and most people would consider him a secondary character to Sir Edmund Hillary."

"That doesn't exactly disprove my point," Derrick insisted, gently bouncing in place to stay warm.

Shirley squinted, either in thought or from the cold/smoke combination. Cold days always brought out the flavor of the cheap, mass-produced tobacco, like salmon and a nice Chianti. "I don't know. 'Rick Shaw.' Isn't it a little racist?"

"Isn't 'Norgay' kind of homophobic?"

"That doesn't even make sense!" Shirley said, taking another quick hit from her cigarette. She smoked a lot when she was irritated, not just in terms of number of cigarettes but in terms of inhalations per minute. If she had to deal with Derrick on a daily basis, she wouldn't have lived past forty.

"No, but it makes as much sense as your point," Derrick replied. "I mean, a person can construe anything they want to from a…" He trailed off, either because he lost his place or because he didn't care to finish. "Jesus, you're supposed to be supportive of my ideas." He paused for effect. "You used to be."

Instead of screaming, *THERE IS NO IDEA IN THAT MASS OF SHIT YOU GAVE ME,* Shirley sighed. He was right… sort of…

about one thing. When there weren't contracts to be negotiated, literary agents were equal parts therapist and cheerleader. Art isn't banking, and people have to believe in the project they're pouring their lives into. You have to *make* them believe. If she was a cheerleader, though, she hadn't had much to cheer about lately, and when one of her clients approached her with an idea that still needed several days in the oven before it reached half-baked status, that made her more mopey, not less. Still, getting pissed off at someone who, only a few short years ago, was her most promising client certainly wouldn't change the situation for the better. "I just think your failing to realize that one character name isn't an idea you can build an entire novel around; it's just a detail," she said in an Oscar-worthy impersonation of a calm person. "And I still think it's vaguely racist. I mean, why don't you give him a magical Negro?"

"It's not like he's Chinese," Derrick said, although for a second, his eyes rotated skyward as he obviously entertained the idea of making the character Chinese. He shook his head to clear the thought. "And what's a magical Negro?"

"It's a clichéd plot device," she informed him. "If you want the exemplar, watch *The Legend of Bagger Vance*." She neglected to add, *If you can.*

Derrick nodded, filing the idea away for later. "Look," he said, "I don't know what the name's supposed to mean... yet." He noticed Shirley casually glancing at her watch as her hand drifted past her face on its way to scratching her hairline. "Am I keeping you from a prior engagement?"

Shirley shrugged. "I bumped another meeting for this," she lied. This conversation actually fit in nicely with her non-regulation, half-hour smoke break. She let him step outside with her so they could finish the conversation that had started in her office; much to her professional chagrin, she didn't have another meeting for three hours. In truth, she just didn't like talking to Derrick. It felt like talking to a robot programmed by a drunken person.

"For me?" he asked, slightly uncomfortable. He didn't like having things done for him; it was a major issue for his main character in his unpublished novel, *Thirsty Dog*. It appeared as though he was dipping into that particular well again on his latest opus. It happened: Stephen King rarely left Maine. Chuck Palahniuk floated back and forth between cults and self-help groups. It was a fact that writers liked to visit old haunts; they just usually brought along more than a name-change on subsequent trips. He scratched his chin and looked down. "You didn't have to do that."

"I know I didn't have to," Shirley said, almost defensively, "but I thought you had something."

He shook his head. "No," he said, his tone instantaneously turning more pathetic, "this was more of a pop-in than anything." No one wearing army jacket should look that submissive.

"Derrick, you don't call a trip from New Orleans to New York a pop-in," Shirley insisted. "You make that trip for a reason. At least most people do."

"I am; I'm catching a flight out of JFK to Korea."

"North or South?" she asked, hopefully. If it was North Korea, that would be a win-win situation for her: either he would come out of that experience with a hell of a book, or Kim Jung Un would have him killed or abducted she wouldn't have to deal with him anymore.

"South. I'm running a marathon in Seoul."

She nodded, trying not to look too disappointed now that his survival was all but guaranteed. "You don't speak Korean, do you?"

"I've learned how to say 'thank you' and 'excuse me,' which I've found gets me through about seventy-percent of situations when I'm traveling to foreign lands." He shook his head. "It doesn't matter, though: like, every fifth person there is U.S. military personnel."

"How in god's name do you afford these trips?" she asked. She liked to think of herself as something of a sophisticate, but other than a trip to Frankfort, Germany, for a book fair, she hadn't left the country at all during the last year. Hell, she hadn't left the Five Boroughs in the last five months.

"I have a job," he countered, referring to a temp job he had since October, working as a security guard on one of the docks along Lake Pontchartrain, "and I'm still getting residuals off of my books."

Shirley scoffed, but turned it into a smoker's hack in time to save face. In truth, Derrick was still getting significant residuals from *a* book, not books. He wrote the novel, *Dead Man in Sheets*, over ten years ago. Although Shirley never bothered to read it when it came out, it did make several "book of the year" lists, no doubt partly due to him being twenty-one at the time, and everyone expected that book to be the tip of the literary iceberg. It wasn't, though; it was just some random ice. He wrote five books since then, and they were all shit. Not even weird-cult-classic, William Burroughs shit; just boring, pointless, rambling, self-indulgent shit. She'd seen it happen before, where an author finds some success and starts to take himself too seriously. Shirley typically didn't care, though, even when it was her client. It was enough if a client wrote one great book that sold well enough to appear in airport book stores; she'd put together the paperwork and take her cut of the sales, and everyone would be happy. The problem with Derrick, and a major reason why she secretly hated him, was that he wrote and published *Dead Man in Sheets* with no agent.

That's right: the little weirdo wrote his version of a goddamn literary masterpiece while working the night shift at the 7 Eleven. He says he actually wrote most of it *at* work, after the three a.m. rush of customers looking to buy alcohol and condoms had subsided. Furthermore, he got it published with no representation, after sending it to a mere five publishers and using a cover letter that misspelled "peruse." As much as a small part of her admired the Horatio Algerness of it all, the details of Derrick's saga pissed off the rest of her. It made her feel irrelevant... if not something of an artistic impediment. She only stumbled into her current occupation after failing as a writer, and as if that epic, soul-sucking disaster didn't provide a big enough kick in the taco, as an agent, she somehow couldn't guide this universally acknowledged "talent" to find his muse a second time.

Shirley flicked the spent cigarette over the ledge, confident that it would extinguish before it landed on a pedestrian. She had serious problems, though, problems a lot more concrete than a bruised ego; her job at the agency was in jeopardy. She needed her authors to produce in order for her to justify occupying a desk, and god help her, Derrick was still her most famous client. With *Dead Man* not their property, though, they had made little more off him than the percentage on the advance of his other, mediocre efforts. That's why she hated talking to Derrick (well... one reason), but that's also why she got excited when he called her a couple days ago and told her he was coming to the city for a visit: after months of getting 'faced down in New Orleans, she thought he might have finally wandered into a semi-marketable idea. Instead, all he had was "Rick Shaw" and a worm saddle. It was a bad joke.

Shirley put her hands in the pockets of her black, knee-length pea coat, badly wanting another cigarette but wanting to get back inside and wave goodbye to Derrick ten times worse. "Hey, maybe if you pop over to China, you can get some ideas for your Rick Shaw book."

"I thought you said that was racist," he said, squinting against the late winter wind. A thin film of eyelashes failed to keep his eyes from watering.

"Yeah, you're right," she said, turning toward the door. "Good luck in your marathon. How long's this one?"

"26.2 miles," he said without changing expression. "They're all 26.2 miles."

*   *   *

"And then he says, 'They're all 26.2 miles,'" Shirley said to the woman across the table. Her left hand fidgeted as though it had been holding a cigarette that suddenly had disappeared. She was too young to remember those black-and-white commercials where actors playing doctors touted the comparative advantages of certain cigarettes over others, but she felt like a dinosaur for being able to reminisce about being about to smoke in restaurants, back before society decided to quarantine you like some Ebola survivor. Jesus. The Ebola Virus. Was she dating herself again?

"They are?" Samantha said, dressed in a pastel pantsuit and a string of pearls. They were nearly the same age, but Samantha was significantly more "Gatsby" than Shirley. "That's funny. I thought they could go up to, like, 100 miles."

"He mentioned something about the distance being based on a guy running from the city of Marathon during the Peloponnesian Wars." Since she couldn't smoke, Shirley took a sip of water. The restaurant used long-stemmed goblets for water glasses, but they held a surprisingly large volume of ice and water. "It was something like a five-minute explanation, but I tuned out after 'Peloponnesian.'"

"That's kind of neat that he runs those things," Samantha said, picking at the remains of her salad, the bits that she hadn't slathered with ranch dressing. They sat in a brightly lit café with white tablecloths and a big bay window that looked more like the type of place that would (a) feature a large patio and (b) be located in L.A., but it possessed neither attribute. It looked out of place in New York, among the population clad in their black-and-gray woolen outfits, but Samantha liked to go there whenever she was feeling California. She felt that way today, what with spring right around the corner. "Most writers just drink."

"Derrick drinks recreationally, but mainly, he pops pills and runs marathons." Shirley took a sip out of her porcelain coffee cup, privately wondering if some day they would outlaw the drinking of coffee inside; it left stains, after all. She caught herself before she felt *too* persecuted; the yellow stains and the tar buildup weren't the reason cigarettes were criminalized, it was the respiratory damage they inflicted on innocent bystanders. "He lives this bizarre life that doesn't go anywhere, but he can afford to, all because of some flash-in-the-pan success he had when he was in college. I guess you don't have to be talented to be eccentric."

"Oh, I think he's talented," Samantha said, downing the remains of her second glass of lunch wine. Shirley didn't have to worry about Sam getting pickled to the point of sabotaging the conversation; that girl could drink. In fact, Samantha kept a fifth of Smirnoff in her desk drawer to top off her Diet Cokes. She wasn't real secretive about it, either, always offering to share (bless her heart) with any non-supervisors in the office. "I read a couple of the one's he's had us represent him on, and I thought they were quite good stories. Inaccessible, maybe, but at least interesting."

"Inaccessible-but-interesting doesn't move product," Shirley reminded her co-worker. "I tried to get him to focus on what he did with

Dead Man... not re-write it and change the setting and character names, like Dan Brown does, but just get a feel for how readable it was... but he said that book 'represented a phase' that he had passed through." She shook her head and looked out the window in time to see a young woman walk past wearing a red leather jacket and an aristocratic bearing. It made Shirley feel a little nostalgic; even though she never would have worn a red leather jacket in public, there was a time when she could have, and now that time is gone. "He came to me today, and all he had was the name of the protagonist: Rick Shaw."

Sam squinted. "The guy who invented the set?"

Shirley's face puckered into an identical expression. "Come again?"

"You know, like in volleyball: bump-set-spike," Same told her. "Rick Shaw was the guy who invented the set."

Shirley shook her head, privately wondering how one "invents" hitting the volleyball upward with your fingers. "No... and how the hell do you know this?"

"Julie Kane," Sam said, referencing one of her clients. "She wrote a book on the history of California beach sports." She smiled, whimsically, "It's funny, the random shit you learn in this business."

"Hmm. It sure is," Shirley said, privately wishing she had more clients who wrote nonfiction. "Derrick might be better off basing his book around that guy's life, but god knows he's probably not in 'that phase,' either." She sighed. "Sometimes he reminds me of one of those choir boys who hits puberty, then his voice changes and makes him useless."

Samantha kept smiling the smile of someone with a secure job as her eyes took on a distant, slightly intoxicated depth. "Yeah, the way I hear it, you could really use him... *finding his voice* again."

Shirley's eyebrows crawled up her forehead if to say *ain't that the truth*, but they stopped in mid-arch. "Um, what did you hear, exactly?"

"Well, it's not exactly a secret that we're in a recession," Samantha said, shrugging and glancing at her empty wine glass. Her eyes drifted to the ornate clock on the wall with the gold hands as she contemplated the time it would take to order and consume one more glass of wine. "And obviously, the publishing industry is getting hit as hard as anything... people just don't read anymore, what with the Tweeting and the reality TV... and Doug's looking to unload anything he thinks is dead weight—"

"I'm dead weight?" Shirley said, a little too loudly for public discourse. The café was half-empty (although Samantha undoubtedly would describe it as half-full), so the sound carried unnervingly far. None of their fellow patrons turned and looked, but most of them considered it. "That's what you're telling me?" she said shifting to her inside-voice.

"No," Samantha said, reflexively, her eyes widening as her glossy lips pursed, "but you might start *resembling* dead weight if you don't find a winner soon."

"Jesus Christ," Shirley muttered, shaking her head. "Jesus Christ. I mean, I know things haven't been good..."

"Don't take it personally," Samantha said. With another friend, she might have reached across the table and touched the friend's hand for support. Shirley wasn't the sort of person you did that with, though, and they didn't have that sort of relationship. "These things are cyclical. No one thinks you're dragging the agency down, but Doug has to act like he's being proactive."

"He's just using it as a cudgel to do something he's wanted to do for a long time." Shirley snorted without looking up from the empty bread basket on the table. "'Don't take it personally.' That's easy for you to say. You're not the one—"

"Can I get you ladies anything, or are you ready for the check?" asked the Latina waitress with the too-perfect boobs who materialized next to Shirley's chair. Shirley's outburst probably summoned her.

"Both," Shirley said before Samantha could. "She'll have another White Zin and I'll have a double martini, dirty. And I'll take the check." Starting tomorrow, she could act like a charity case, but for today, she was still paying for lunch.

"I don't know if I should," Samantha said, tilting her head, offering the token resistance that Shirley was obligated to knock down.

"It's for me," Shirley assured her, "because I'm not drinking alone." The waitress finished scribbling the simplest order in the world down on her notepad, confirming to Shirley that she didn't have that job for her table-waiting skills, then smiled and scurried off. When she had retreated out of earshot, Shirley proceeded to take the Lord's name in vain for the third time in one minute.

"Relax" Samantha said, the way one can only when one is slightly drunk and just optioned a client's novel about sky-diving bank-robbers for a film starring Paul Walker. "These things always work themselves out." Shirley hated pointless, condescending advice, but telling Samantha to shove it would alienate one of the few friends and allies within the agency that Shirley still had left. Self-control proved immediately fortuitous, too, because the next sentence would change the course of Shirley's life forever. "Besides," Samantha said with a shrug, "maybe the North Koreans will shoot down Derrick's plane and all his books will start selling like crazy."

As her eyes tracked the droplet of condensation descending down her water class, Shirley calculated how long her savings would last if she couldn't get another job. For some reason, the experience created the sensation of drowning. Then, Samantha's statement registered in her brain and she asked, "What?"

"Well, usually, it's a good career move for artists to die prematurely, like Jim Morrison or Kurt Cobain… or Marilyn Monroe," Samantha explained, waving a hand, casually. "It adds to their mystique when we never get to see them grow old or start embarrassing themselves."

"Eh," Shirley said. "For rock stars and actors, maybe; they have to stay beautiful. But authors… nobody cares if they get old because nobody knows what they look like. And Derrick already embarrasses himself."

"Well what about John Kennedy O'Toole?"

"*A Confederacy of Dunces* was a wonderful book," Shirley said with all the unbridled passion of an English lit graduate student. "And his name was John Kennedy *Toole*."

"It was a wonderful book," Samantha acknowledged, conspicuously scanning the environs to see how soon that third glass of wine would be arriving. To her credit, she didn't get pissy at being corrected, "but it didn't sell… didn't even get published… until, what? Ten years after he'd died?" Sam continued with the story that they both knew, about how Toole's mother got the book published ten years after his death and it won the Pulitzer Prize (or maybe it was the National Book Award), but she really didn't have to, because the seed of the idea had already started to simultaneously bloom in Shirley's mind: if something happened to someone like Derrick, it would make at least the national news, and sales for his books would increase. And maybe, just maybe, the details of his weird little life would surface, and he would look like some kind of tortured genius, and the sales would really take off.

Shirley settled back in her thinly cushioned, iron chair. A hum started emanating through her body that almost seemed audible. She'd originally just thought of Derrick's death as removing a punishment, but it could produce some real rewards. It was a long-shot, but working toward a goal always helped focus Shirley. In fact, she felt so good that, when the drinks arrived, she celebrated by eating the olives in her martini, in direct defiance of the social stigma against people who eat garnish.

* * *

Chapter Two:

K is for "Kontract Killer"

"Rob? Hi, it's Shirley," Shirley said into the mouthpiece of the landline phone sitting on her desk. It was an older, black plastic, two-line phone, but it didn't look out of place amid the eclectic clutter of her great, wooden desk. She kept pillars of paper littered about its surface and atop her many shelves. The specifications of the pillars reflected her organizational system: They had to be high enough to conserve space, but low enough that she could see the top page, because if she couldn't identify something at a glance, it might as well disappear from existence for the near future. She topped each stack with a fist-sized rock or, when she ran out of those, assorted office bric-a-brac (e.g., stapler, scotch tape dispenser) to keep them from blowing away in the drafty office. It was an effective system, just as long as she stayed under about twenty stacks.

"Hey, Shirley," Rob said, sounding a little groggy because it was 8:30 in the morning in Tacoma. Then again, Rob always sounded groggy. He had one of those voices, like Tom Waits, that sounded like he'd smoked two packs of cigarettes and drank a fifth of whiskey the night before... although in Tom Waits' case, he probably had drank and smoked that much. "Haven't heard from you in a while. To what do I owe the pleasure?"

"I just like to check in with my clients from time to time," she lied. In truth, she couldn't get yesterday's conversation with Samantha out of her head, and it was bugging her enough to warrant inflicting an 8:30 a.m. phone call on someone. She actually hated calling most of her clients unless she had something positive to say to them; they were such a neurotic group, who knew whether the next piece of bad news would send them into a depression spiral? Rob wasn't like that, though; he was the sort who just got a charge out of seeing his name in print. It made him feel like an intellectual in a world of luddites. He owned a company that manufactured aircraft parts (or distributed them... she was never clear on the details), so his lifestyle would maintain the same level of relative comfort if his book sold fifty copies or fifty thousand. He was more of a writing hobbyist than one of those "artists" who poured their soul out on the page, who lived and died with each manuscript submission. Shirley used to be an "artist," but like her father told her: You gotta grow up some time. Of course, ol' Dad's blunt pragmatics probably contributed to his dying bitter and alone... but that was another story. "So, what are you working on these days?"

"Same as last time," he said, voice thinning as he probably stretched a muscular arm over his head. "Finishing up the third book of the *Countdown to Zero* series." She imagined him tying a terrycloth bathrobe with one hand as he spoke, the wiry hares of his chest pocking through the open "V." He was the kind of man who aged well, like Josh Brolin. Maybe it had to do with bone structure, or the fact that there wasn't a lot of sunlight in Washington to age the skin. Also like Josh Brolin, he was happily married to a lovely woman.

"Great," she said, trying to hit that octave where she sounded excited, then lied again, "I can't wait to read it." Rob wrote books that were, for lack of a better phrase, cheap knock-offs of the old TV series *24*. Unlike *24*, the *Countdown to Zero* books weren't an overt right-winger's wet dream; Rob had gone to great pains not to use any Arab villains up to this point. Because of this (or maybe in spite of it), people liked the books enough that he was able to turn it into a series. What his stories lacked in artistic flourish, they made up for in detail, courtesy of his business contacts with defense contractors.

"Yeah, in this one, I have Jeff Brower taking on Quebecois separatists who are smuggling a dirty bomb into San Francisco."

"Sounds exciting," Shirley said, badly wanting to add *if not terribly coherent*. Exactly how would irradiating San Francisco bring about Quebec's independence? "You gotta be careful, though: with that target, the neo-cons in your audience might be rooting for the Quebecois to succeed."

"Hm, really didn't consider that," he admitted, the stubble of his salt-and-pepper beard grating against the phone mouthpiece. "Maybe it'll make the villains less sympathetic. Otherwise, I set this story a year in the future, because I needed a romantic interest and I figured that Jeff would need some time to get over the fact that his fiancé was a sleeper agent working for the Mexican Drug cartels."

"Sounds exciting," Shirley said again, shifting in her ergonomic office chair. She really should get to the point of her call before Rob drank his morning coffee and got his version of the creative juices flowing. He might start waxing poetic about the Basque Nationals or the Wegars. "Listen, Rob, I have a question about *Countdown to Zero II*: how did you get your information about the mercenaries that Dominic Trask hired to kill Jeff? You had a lot of detail in there, and it seemed authentic."

"First of all, that was *Countdown I*," he corrected her, "but you're right: it was totally authentic. I got the intel from a guy I used to know who worked for Greystone Unlimited… or at least one of their front companies."

"Do you still have the contact information for the guy?" Shirley asked, casually. Somehow, she could sense Rob bristle on the other end of the line and knew what was coming next.

"Seems like a strange request. Care to elaborate?" He sounded like one of the two-dimensional characters from his books.

"One of my authors is writing a book featuring contract killers," she said automatically, not needing to consult her notepad. She'd prepped for that question; it was the first one she thought of after she decided to call Rob. She knew Rob fashioned himself as deeper into the cloak & dagger world than he actually was (in her admittedly uninformed opinion), so it was always possible that, after bragging about the scads of information he had, he would say something like, "I'm afraid I can't divulge that information at this juncture," in order to sound mysterious. She also knew, though, that if she emphasized "contract killers," he wouldn't feel as though this mysterious writer was threatening his market niche.

"These people aren't technically contract killers, technically," he informed her, no doubt wondering if she ever bothered to actually *read* his books. "I mean, some of them handle an odd hit from an outside employer once in a while, but it's not like they unionize. Any activity like that is strictly off the books."

Christ, he made them sound like cops moonlighting as security guards. She especially enjoyed the choice of "activity" as a euphemism for "killing people for money." She usually reserved the term "activity" for kindergarteners using safety scissors and paste. "Be that as it may," she said, "I'm sure this would be something your contact could enlighten me on."

"Who is the author you're doing all this legwork for?" Rob asked, almost chuckling. "You got a kid who decided he wants to break into the literary business or something?" It was Shirley's turn to stifle a scoff, either because she never thought she presented herself as particularly nurturing or motherly, or because *Countdown to Zero* and its offspring were about as "literary" as the text accompanying the maze on the back of a Denny's placemat. Before she could cobble together a palatable response, Rob added, "*Countdown 1* was five years ago, though; I have no idea where that guy is… or even if he's still alive."

Then what's with the defensive smokescreens? she wanted to yell. He did everything but warn her that he could give her the name and phone number of the contact, but that he would have to kill her. She suspected the answer, though: he was lying about the credentials of his mysterious contact, and she couldn't call him out on it, because unlike Derrick, copies of Rob's books still sold… *multiple* copies. "I understand. Well, thanks anyway, Rob," she forced herself to say. "Good to hear from you." Her hand traced down the "Rob Martin" page of her open notebook. "Say 'hi' to Brenda and Tyler."

"Will do," he replied, then hung up and probably went back to his bedroom to make sweet love to his wife.

*   *   *

The idea of hiring a contract killer struck Shirley as a bit of a reach, even when it first dawned on her, but examining all your options never hurt. It just made sense to cross the most direct solutions off the list *before* descending into some Rube-Goldberg-type plan. There was a simple beauty in driving a stake through the heart of the problem: make a phone call, wire money, wait for a confirmation, then wire more money. It was so modern and efficient, just like ordering a pizza, except that you go through an unregistered account in the Cayman Islands instead of just using a Visa card. It probably worked out for the best, though, that Rob was full of shit. She really wasn't equipped to deal with people from that world; she'd spent her whole life working in air conditioned offices.

In fact, she really didn't know whether she wanted to off Derrick, but she was curious about the going rate for that sort of "activity," what with knowledge being power and so on. Doing it herself certainly wasn't an option; she didn't have the starch for assassination. Hell, emptying the rat trap in her office made her weepy and useless for an entire day. She leaned over her keyboard and stared at the empty Google search bar. You can't exactly do an internet search for "contract killers," and if you search "assassins," you'd probably end up with links to a video game or that gawd awful movie with Antonio Banderas. You also might end up on a Homeland Security watch list. She could search for the schematics of a car and probably deduce how to cut someone's break line, but out of control cars caused a lot of collateral damage. Besides, Derrick didn't seem like the sort who owned a car. As far as she could tell, he only drove when making cross-country trips… which didn't currently apply since he would be in South Korea for the next couple weeks.

The thoughts of South Korea naturally drifted toward thoughts of smoking; people smoked like chimneys over there. The digital clock in the lower right-hand corner of her computer screen indicated that it was almost noon. Almost time for her pre-lunch smoke break. She would hold off, though, and use it as a reward… a tar-laced carrot, if you will. If she could come up with one decent idea about how to drastically increase Derrick's chances of an untimely fatality, she would allow herself to go enjoy a nice, long smoke. It was called "delay of gratification," and it was something successful people were good at. She tapped the plastic cap of her complimentary Hyatt pen on the edge of her desk, then stuck the undoubtedly filthy pen-cap-end into the corner of her mouth. There had to be some workable strategy that existed in the vast gulf between the direct route of hiring someone to shoot Derrick in the back of the head and the passive route of including his death in her nightly prayers.

Like the flame from a cheap butane lighter, the idea ignited in her head and started to build momentum with each passing second, filling the space in her plan like a fiery puzzle piece (Shirley tended to mix metaphors when preoccupied). Derrick liked to do stupid, random things, whether they involved recreational drug use, running marathons in northeast Asia, or donating his entire paycheck to the Save the Koalas Foundation. He wasn't the world's most stable person, and she could see from the manuscripts he'd been sending her that his world view had become progressively darker since their initial year together. Maybe if she just gave him a nudge, or a series of nudges, in the right direction, it might land him in a place where doing something irrational seemed like a legitimately good idea. If Jim Jones could convince nine hundred semi-normal, good-natured people to drink cyanide, surely Shirley could make one introverted weirdo throw himself in front of a bullet train. She just had to perform the delicate dance of mustering the entirety of her nudging ability, yet keeping her motivations disguised…

Smoke break!

*   *   *

Chapter Three:

Flight of the Cyborg

Rick Shaw used both hands to shove closed the heavy door of his recently manufactured car. The latch clicked, and he took a moment to lean against the car and expel a weary sigh. He never liked going to Chinatown, probably because everyone assumed he did. It wasn't the sort of joke that went away the longer he stayed in the homicide/vice department, because every new fish they hired on the force always fancied himself the first comedian to make that connection the moment he heard Rick's name. The same, lame joke lingered in the air of the station house like a specter, waiting for the sound of his name to summon it forth. After ten years on the job, you'd think that it wouldn't be the first thing his co-workers thought about when they thought of him, but on many days, you'd be wrong.

Rick crouched down to get a better new of the crime scene, privately wondering how in the hell the criminals committed that particular crime in that particular location. "O'Kelly," he called out in a low, clear voice without taking his eyes off the particular section of crime scene, "get over here."

Sergeant O'Kelly descended from one or more generations of cops in the city. He knew every inch of the town, from the neighborhoods near the local body of water all

the way over to the proper name for the urban manufacturing center. He was a good
cop. Rick trusted him, but even good cops made mistakes. "What can I do fah you,
Detective Shaw?" He said, bracing his slightly pudgy hands on his slightly knobby
knees as he lowered himself, gingerly, bringing his eyelevel closer to Rick's. His patent
leather belt wheezed like a set of truck brakes.

Rick pointed a gloved finger toward the discordant detail of the crime scene.
"Can you explain to me what that's doing here?"

O'Kelly's red-rimmed eyes widened to the point where the threatened to pop
out of their sockets. "Faith and begorah! How did we miss that? We'll have the boys
at the lab(?) check on it fahst thing, Detective."

"You do that and call me and let me know the results," Rick said, his knees
popping as they lifted him out of his crouch. He didn't blame O'Kelly for slipping
up… because it wasn't a slip-up; that wasn't the kind of clue you could miss, not even
if you were trying to. That meant that someone had planted it there in the last couple
minutes, someone still close by, someone who was trying to send him a message. Rick
removed his iPhone from the pocket of his trench coat (or walked to the nearest rotary
phone); he had some calls to make.

*   *   *

Derrick hated flying. He wasn't phobic about it; he knew the
favorable statistics and had no moral compunctions about humans being
borne aloft by mechanical means. He hated it in the same way that he
hated domestic beer. As with domestic beer, there were obvious
advantages of flying. For example, domestic beer was cheap. Similarly,
after he made it through the exhaustive body-cavity-search that post-9-11
airport security had become, he found most non-Chicago-O'Hare airports
quite relaxing; they had coffee and booze and usually allowed him to sit
and do nothing but read or write. On the downside, domestic beer tasted
worse than Listerine (literally), and the cramped and uncomfortable
airplane seats made sleeping almost impossible. The headrests never lined

up with his head, and when the seat in front of him reclined, it felt like someone had entombed him in a Z-shaped coffin. The only workable strategy he had developed over the years involved taking a morphine tablet shortly after takeoff. With one of those down his gullet, he could practically sleep standing up, but on flights less than six hours, the combination left him too high to drive after the plane landed.

Drinking domestic beer and flying coach also both highlighted his lack of financial success: if he'd written a best-seller or something that got turned into a movie, he could have afforded to sit in first class, where he could have knocked back a couple glasses of Pino Noir, sprawled out in one of those fully-reclining pods during long, international flights, and got blowjobs from stewardesses… at least that's what he imagined first class was like. Instead, along with the rest of the cattle, he passed by those forever unattainable seats on his way to Economy Class, envy burning in his eyes at the sight of the middle-aged white men filling the pods with their fat asses, golf shirts, and Wall Street Journals. In his mind, they all worked for Lockheed Martin and were traveling to a conference in Qatar on how to maximize your war profiteering.

Derrick sat in an aisle seat, toward the middle of the cabin, adjacent to the wing, but not in an emergency exit row. Airlines charged more for the emergency exit row these days, which struck Derrick as pathetic evidence of the declining comfort of modern air travel; getting chosen for exit rows used to be like impressment. Now, some people would claw out the eyes of a fellow passenger to get that extra six inches of knee space. He preferred the aisle to the window because he liked to get up and use the lavatory at least once per flight; moving around supposedly reduced one's chances of developing blood clots and, in turn, getting strokes… plus, he had a small bladder. When he got stuck with the window seat, that still had its perks: he could at least lean his head against the hard plastic wall and go to sleep. No one preferred the middle seat… except maybe frotteurists.

He kept his army jacket on while seated, still not fully adjusting to the north Atlantic weather after his months in New Orleans. A woman sat in the seat to his immediate right, but he actually felt a little lucky when the cabin door closed, because across the aisle, one lone guy sat in a block of four seats. The guy had a head of shaggy, curly hair mashed under a camouflage baseball cap, and an equally unwieldy girth trapped under a plain white T-shirt. He looked like a character from the show *30 Rock*, and, for the life of him, Derrick couldn't imagine why this guy was flying to Tokyo. When the cabin door slid closed with its muffled thud, Derrick slid across the aisle and into one of the empty seats; it struck him as basic math: now he, the lady in the window seat and the guy two seats away would all have a pair of seats in which to stretch out. As Derrick fastened his seat belt low and tight across his lap, he glimpsed the guy in the baseball cap conspicuously staring at him. "Hi," Derrick said and squeezed out a tight-lipped smile.

"Did you pay for that seat?" the guy asked.

"No," Derrick said, neglecting to ask, *Did you?*

"Well, I was going to stretch out…," the guy informed him, even though he looked like he'd have to stretch his stubby, sausage-finger hands over his head in order to fully occupy all four seats.

Derrick thought of several logical arguments to justify his position, but he was starting to get angry, and when that happened, the most palatable responses became the ones where he yelled "Fuck you!" and punched the guy in his fat face (not that he actually did that, but it always seemed like a *really* good idea). That would get him kicked off the plane, and he would probably end up on a No Fly list, and he would miss his marathon. Besides, he hated… *hated* getting angry; it made him feel out of control and… shaken(?) for a couple hours afterward. So, instead, the only form of protest he allowed himself involved staring at the guy and asking, "Seriously?"

"Yeah," the guy said defiantly.

Derrick knew that, if he raised a stink, the flight attendants probably would side with him, but then he and his possessions, including the laptop computer that constituted 90% of his life, would be stuck next to this asshole for thirteen hours, so in the name of harmony, he unbuckled his seatbelt, muttered, "Fine, asshole," and crossed back over to his seat. Crisis averted. Suppression saves the day again… but for the next thirteen hours, he knew he would have to block out the image of dirty socks hovering a few feet away as the guy lowered his cap over his eyes, splayed himself across his row of seats, and intermittently slept. Each time, Derrick would have to re-convince himself that he did the right thing.

*   *   *

Soon, the plane lifted into the air, the fasten seatbelt sign turned off, and a pair of grey sweat socks with blue, horizontal stripes hovered a few feet to Derrick's left. As was so often the case, Derrick coped with distress through distraction. He typed out about a page of his new novel on the laptop, then deleted that first page. After an hour of work, he had only an empty screen staring back at him to show for it. He really needed to get some work done because the laptop battery only had about one hour of juice left, but he just couldn't have Rick Shaw work in Chinatown; it was too on-the-nose to be clever, and a detective novel set in Chinatown would invariably descend into a derivative soup of some combination of *Chinatown* or *Big Trouble in Little China*. Even he was better than that.

He took a deep breath of the recycled airplane air. That was one of his major problems, writing-wise: he was usually better than his ideas. Everything used to be easier and more acceptable. Ten years ago, he indulged in an idea because he liked it, but after *Dead Man* hit the jackpot, he had to show he was maturing as a writer, and every phrase in every sentence carried that added weight of what high school English teachers the world over would think. The commercial failure of his four follow-up books magnified this burden, and as he stared at the blinking cursor on the white page, his precarious existence in the literary world seldom felt less stable.

Derrick did not love his life, but he had grown content with its simple pleasures. He was lonely, self-consciously so, but on the other hand, he could work jobs with minimal responsibility and quit them whenever they got too tedious. He could afford to pay for the occasional trans-Pacific plane ticket, health insurance, and a steady but modest supply of recreational drugs. With the passing years, though, the royalties had gotten smaller and smaller. When the stream turned into a trickle, the good parts of his life would dry up along with it. He was also getting older, entering that creepy life phase that comes around shortly after the ten-year high school reunion, when people you hadn't spoken to or thought of in more than a decade contact you using social networking sites to see what you've been up to. These attempts at contact always included personal updates that he didn't ask for. Karl and Michelle got married. Ted is a partner at the firm. Joan had twins named Molly and Polly. These advertisements of maturation made him feel like his life should be heading somewhere, anywhere instead of gradually down.

He always tried real freaking hard to write something good. Some of the jobs he took, like hospital janitor and nightclub bouncer, he took just because it provided him with what he hoped would be book-worthy anecdotes. He ended up with some weird stories, but like a failed skin-graft, they just wouldn't take… for whatever reason. Inspiration wasn't *all* perspiration, though; sometimes, you can get caught up in the details and lose sight of the big picture. That's the main reason why he was making this trip he really couldn't afford: to run, to get that ol' endorphin rush, to unplug from the recent lockstep of his life, to see a part of the world he never had, and to discover whether some combination of these experiences could help him tell the story of a mysterious man with the unfortunate name of Rick Shaw.

"You'll run down your battery doing that," the woman in the window seat told Derrick. She had been sleeping, or attempting to, for the initial hour of the flight. She was Asian, and the flight was headed to Tokyo, so the fact that she spoke flawless English surprised him a little bit.

"Doing what?" he asked in a flat monotone. His voice constituted one of his most recognizable characteristics, like Sherlock Holmes' pipe. He didn't like it, or the fact that people down at the dock where he worked in New Orleans called him "Lurch," like the mutant butler from the *Addam's Family*, but unnatural, deliberate vocal inflection sounded even more idiotic than the monotone. A bad voice is like bad posture: the harder you try to fix it, the more fake it comes off.

"Not doing anything but leaving it on," she replied in a voice that subtly changed intonation with each syllable that rolled off her tongue in a way that made him slightly jealous. She was small and cute, with an unknown amount of black hair tied into a bun that exposed her graceful neck. Several years (in his favor) probably separated them, but age was hard to detect on Asian women, so he didn't feel like a pervert while coveting her. "Then, when you finally know what to do with it, you won't have any battery life."

"It helps me think," Derrick lied. Blank screens didn't help him think. If anything, they taunted him and made him more apprehensive, but he always became reflexively defensive whenever people told him how to act. Plus, he thought that sounded clever.

The young woman shrugged. "Suit yourself," she said and returned to her paperback novel.

A part of Derrick that was not work-obsessed wanted to continue the conversation… god knows the last time he spoke with an attractive woman who wasn't serving him coffee… but couldn't think of anything organic to say. *Pretend you're a normal person,* he told himself. *Pretend your Joe Normal, a completely mundane character in a shallow, vacuous story.* "What are you reading?" he asked. He read and traveled a lot, so that and "where are you from?" were about the only icebreakers for which he could manage a follow-up. The fact that she was reading (and not listening to an iPod) actually gave him options. As long as it wasn't a Harry Potter book, he might be able to sustain a conversation with this lovely creature for a few minutes, and who knows? Maybe, against all odds, she would find his grinding, clanging social skills quirky instead of creepy, and they would exchange first names, and if she had a layover in Tokyo, too, they could run off together to a distant unisex restroom for a romantic interlude.

"*Twilight*," she replied, holding up the cover that showed something red in front of a black background.

"Oh, never mind," he said and returned his attention to his blank computer screen. For some reason, an emptiness crept into his gut. That feeling always overtook him in the wake of failure. Did it constitute a failure because he didn't get what he wanted or because he couldn't even bring himself to try? He didn't know which it was, but that didn't matter, because emotions aren't logical. So, even if he found the source of his discomfort, he couldn't rationalize his way out of it. He just knew that he wouldn't be getting that romantic interlude. As always, his thoughts had sprinted ahead of him, building castles in the air despite lacking both mortar and brick.

*   *   *

The first in-flight movie was some piece of tripe featuring the guy from *Magic Mike* and the girl from *Mama Mia!* The second movie had something to do with the guy who invented the windshield wiper. Derrick wasn't interested in either of them, but when his laptop battery died, he finally broke down, unwrapped the headset, and watched the second half of the second movie (it made no impression). After that, he fell into a merciful sleep that he would have sworn lasted an hour, but when he woke up and checked the big-faced watch on the dirty wrist of the selfish loser across the aisle, only eight minutes had passed. If he wanted a real nap, he'd have to pop one of the half-dozen morphine tablets stashed in the Dramamine tube in his coat pocket and order a domestic beer.

There are competing schools of thought on drugging yourself during a flight. Some people swear by sleeping pills, but ingesting those just made Derrick tired, they never made him comfortable. His one attempt at using them on a flight left him too exhausted to read or even keep his eyes open, but still dully aching at an 85-degree angle, so he just sat with his eyes closed, mostly awake, for hours on end. Painkillers, on the other hand, made him comfortable to the point to where sitting in an airplane seat felt like lying spread-eagle on a waterbed. There was a third school of thought, of course, that one shouldn't take narcotics on flights (or any other time), but those people were either midgets or masochists.

Derrick's chemical arsenal only provided him with painkillers, so he couldn't have taken sleeping pills even if he wanted to. He had a couple regular connections for pills, but he mostly got them from generous souls here and there who broke a bone and didn't need their refill, or careless hosts who allowed him to use their restroom and didn't bother counting the drugs in their medicine cabinets. It wasn't like he was getting illegal prescriptions from a crooked doctor or buying them on street corners. He had yet to coax a script out of a doctor by complaining about back pain, but with his running history, that option remained available, should he need it. He was putting off that strategy, because so far he had remained safely on the "abuser" side of the abuser/addict dichotomy. Once he turned on that faucet, though, he might have a hard time turning it back off.

Prior to last summer, he probably never had a lethal number of pills on his person at any one time. Last summer, though, fate sent him a work-friend whose roommate was a pharmaceutical rep. The roommate's husband was a drug addict who recently died, and she was disposing of things that reminded her of him, including his big box of painkillers and anxiolytics (and, strangely, boner pills). They all came in pre-packaged form, but Derrick didn't have to pay for a single one.

The second movie had ended, so the flight attendants were conducting another drink service. Derrick craned his neck down the aisle and saw that the closest drink cart had only serviced about three rows of people and wouldn't be arriving for another ten or fifteen minutes. He didn't want to wait that long. It took his mouth about ten seconds to churn up enough saliva for him to swallow the chalky pill in one effortful gulp. As he waited for the drink cart to come back by, as the pill inched down his esophagus, he opened the book that he had jammed in the other pocket of his olive-drab jacket.

"What are you reading?" his cute Asian neighbor asked, speaking for the first time in three hours. She was small enough that she could curl up in her seat like a squirrel and get some real sleep. Thank god it was her sitting there and not someone who stank or weighed 700 pounds.

"*No Man Knows My Name*," Derrick replied without looking up from his book; he didn't want to seem too eager. "It's a book written in the 1950's about the founder of Mormonism."

"Are you a Mormon?" she asked.

"God no," Derrick replied, but quickly shifted his eyes in her direction. She shook her head and held up a hand to assure him that she wasn't offended. "It's pretty fucked up, even for a religion."

"Then why are you reading about it?"

"Because it's pretty fucked up," he explained, replacing the receipt he used to mark the page. "It interests me. When people do strange and bizarre things, I like to find out why." She nodded, but he continued anyway. "I recently read a biography of Heinrich Himmler, but I don't condone what he did; it wasn't a how-to book."

"I see," she said, slowly, her sculpted eyebrows bobbing. "Sounds like you read a lot. You should get a Kindle."

This time, Derrick rotated his torso fully toward her when he said, flatly, "I loathe Kindle."

Her face scrunched up but remained undeniably cute. She was actually something of a sport, considering that he couldn't stop acting like a space alien. "How can anybody that reads hate Kindle?"

He'd had this conversation before, a few times, and in this case, familiarity bred contempt. "I prefer books as a physical thing, that you can hold in your hand. I guess I'm a romantic that way. More importantly, it makes authors more vulnerable to illegal downloads, just like what happened with the music industry, and unlike rock stars, authors can't make up the difference by touring."

"So? People shouldn't write to make money," she said, probably dredging that argument from a poetry class she took at Vasser. "People should write because they love it."

"Well, speaking as a professional writer," he began, and despite himself, felt a pang of self-satisfaction, "I do love it, and I want to keep doing it because it's the only thing I really love doing. And I can't keep doing it if I have to work at Starbucks forty hours a week to keep from starving."

"Wow," she said, ignoring both his argument and his condescending tone, "You're really a professional writer?" She seemed genuinely impressed. He got a little charge out of that, as well, even though she was bound to be horribly let down as soon as she found out she'd never heard of him. "What did you write?"

"A few things. Some of them never even got published," he admitted automatically, trying to mitigate the inevitable disappointment. "The... most *famous* thing I wrote was *Dead Man in Sheets*."

Her eyes lit up. "I've heard of that!" Then, her eyes dimmed as she added, "I think."

"It's okay; you probably haven't," he said quickly, saving her the trouble of pretending. "It wasn't *that* big of a seller, and I wrote it ten years ago."

"Wow," she said again. "How old were you?"

"Around twenty-one. I was still in college."
"That's really impressive."

"Not really," he assured her. "It was more luck than anything. You just happen to send something to someone with decision-making power when they happen to be in a mood that makes them receptive to it. Then, it happens to get released by the right people when there's a market for the story. I haven't been able to write anything since that was remotely successful."

"Still," she said, giving a little smile that showed that she found his position slightly ridiculous, "you wrote something that... I don't know... *thousands* of people enjoyed. That has to count for something."

Derrick blinked. He never understood why people did that. He already had asserted how he felt about the issue. He didn't ask her to feel the same way. He didn't say it was the *right* way to feel. He didn't even ask her to hypothetically feel the same way if she were in his position. He merely had stated his subjective reaction to his subjective experience... and she couldn't let him have that. People never could; they always had to insist that he see the world through the same honey-glazed lens that they did. They couldn't accept the harmless little statement *I'm not satisfied with the way things turned out.* "Were you an English major?" he asked, his eyebrows arching.

"Minor, but that's why I'm going to Japan," she explained, "to teach English at a high school there."

"So, you *do* know what a platitude is?" Oh, that shut her up. She recoiled slightly and her face took on the expression of someone who just got flicked in the nose. She didn't get Derrick, and she wouldn't unless he pretended to be something he wasn't. He smugly went back to reading about Joseph Smith getting killed by a mob in Illinois. Maybe something in the book would inspire him to write something decent, and he could take another shot at grinding out some creativity when they landed in Tokyo, after he bought a Japan-friendly adaptor for his computer.

* * *

CHAPTER FOUR:

ATTACK OF THE GREEN-EYED MONSTER

Rick Shaw held the woman's face in his heavily calloused hands as strands of her something-length, something-colored hair cascaded over them. "What are we going to do, Rick?" she asked in a voice that left her lips in a breathless sigh of resignation. "My husband already knows about us."

"You don't love him," Rick said firmly, not allowing the gaze of her green eyes to leave his own, "so the last thing you're going to do is go back to that house. And I do love you, so the last thing I'm going to do is let you go back to him. Any other choice is on the table."

She half-smiled and closed her hands around his wrists until they separated and allowed her to lean back onto the downy/thin hotel/motel bedspread. Her bosom heaved under her thin, white T-shirt with each anxious breath. "But Trevor's a powerful man. He can hurt us both in so many ways."

Rick followed her onto the bedspread and positioned himself so that the side of her head rested comfortably against his solid shoulder, the kind of shoulder you can only get by doing whatever manual labor job it is that he does. "I'm not worried," Rick assured her without hesitation. "You're forgetting; I'm the guy who did something *extremely difficult in the recent past." His rough hand slid under her oversized T-shirt and crossed her concave stomach that may or may not have someone's child growing in it. "Besides, I'm pretty powerful, too." His left hand plunged southward, caressing her euphemism for vagina as the heat from his euphemism for penis throbbed against her.*

Rapturous moments passed and found her staring at the ceiling. Strangely, writhing atop the bed sheets, being gently brought to climax by Rick Shaw made the woman think of her husband. Not that climaxing reminded her of making love to her husband or that she imagined her husband's snaggle-toothed, whiskey-soaked mouth on her different euphemism for vagina instead of Rick's. But she thought about how this moment was totally, categorically different than anything she experienced with that bastard. The skill, the care, the surrender on both their parts... it all felt so foreign that she started to cry.

Rick raised his head, and his cobalt blue eyes locked onto hers as they hovered over her rumpled T-shirt. "Everything alright?" he asked.

"It's just... it's been so long," she began, but the emotional surge rushed through her so fast that she had trouble finding the words to describe it. "Before you came along...."

"Hey," he said, climbing up from the foot of the bed, probably intending to wrap her in his tanned, muscular arms until she stopped shaking. "Hey. It's okay, you don't have to —"

"I didn't say stop," she said in an even voice.

*   *   *

"I don't think I can write Romance," Derrick's instant message read. It had been a long time since she IM'd someone, but Derrick was somewhere international, so he had to do that through her email account rather than call or send a text message. If the message had arrived two minutes later, Shirley could have responded using the desktop computer in her office, but since she was in the process of stepping into the elevator, she had to use her iPhone.

"No shit," she replied, both aloud and via instant message. No one stood inside the elevator with her, so she could curse at invisible people with impunity. She continued to type: "U haven't had a girlfriend in 8 yrs, and the only reason that 1 went out with u was because she thought u were going to be a millionaire." She hit the character limit and had to split it into two messages, but she finished the entire statement by the time the elevator reached the twenty-fourth floor.

"Jesus," Derrick replied fast enough to indicate that he was using a full-sized computer and not typing with only his thumbs. The next message elaborated. "That's a little harsh. Did your car get vandalized this morning or something?"

Shirley read the message twice, once on either side of the glass door that served as the entrance to the agency. Less than twenty seconds of walking separated her from her office, so she decided to wait to respond until she got there. Derrick was correct about one thing, though: it *was* a little harsh. Brutal judgments like that always reflexively popped into Shirley's head, especially when responding to Derrick. On some core level, human weakness disgusted her, and when she saw people wallowing in their own self-loathing, she felt a burning desire to grab them and shake them out of it even if that meant hurting their feelings. Part of her job, though, involved cheerleading for people with fragile egos. Her challenge now involved making Derrick feel like absolute shit, but to avoid doing it in such an obvious way that he dropped her as an agent. The details of how to accomplish this intricate goal remained very much in flux.

She silently sent a nod of acknowledgement in the direction of her assistant, Kenny, on her way past his desk and into her office. Her desktop computer remained running from the night before, making those electronic churning noises, so she sat down, logged into her email account, and clicked on her instant messenger program. "Sorry," she typed back after the couple-minute delay. "Getting heat from my boss re: author sales, but that's not ur responsibility. What was that girl's name, btb?"

"Sylvia," Derrick wrote back. Shirley was hoping for a last name, but she definitely remembered that Derrick's ex lived in Peoria, IL, and how many Sylvia's could there be from Peoria? Ten? At least now she definitely had the correct spelling; Derrick's anal retentiveness demanded that he proofread and spell-checked all of his instant messages. They read like an AP wire report and totally helped her understand why he never had any success dating over the internet. It also explained why he hated texting. "I wish I could help."

"Well, technically, u can," she typed. "How's ur book coming?"

"Eh," he typed back. "Nothing worth reporting."

"U still basing the entire thing around Rick Shaw?"

"Yes," he replied. Shirley thought he might leave it at that and started to type a reply, but Derrick added, "There's something there. I just have to find it."

Shirley's assistant popped his head, with its ponytail and receding hairline, into her doorway in order to get her attention. He mimed someone drinking out of a cup to inquire whether she wanted a cup of coffee. "Yes, Kenny," she said tonelessly. "I want coffee. I'm not talking on the phone. You don't have to play charades."

"Sorry," Kenny said, dejected, and skulked away, she assumed in the direction of the kitchen.

Shirley shook her head, unable to decide whether Derrick or Kenny annoyed her more. "Y'know he invented the spike?" she typed to Derrick.

"What?" Derrick responded.

"A co-worker informed me that a guy named Rick Shaw invented the spike, like in volleyball," she typed, accidentally butchering the unconfirmed information Samantha had provided her.

"What am I supposed to do with that?" he asked.

"IDK. Idk what ur looking 4 out of this. Is it supposed to be funny?"

"I think it is," he wrote. The nice thing about text messaging with Derrick was that you got the verbal content but didn't miss any of the nonverbal signals (e.g., body language, voice intonation) because he didn't have any.

"But u have a personality disorder," she typed back. "Most people don't find things u think r funny funny."

"You think I have a personality disorder?" he wrote back.

Had Derrick sat in one of the chairs on the other side of her great wooden desk instead of a few thousand miles away, Shirley would have shot him her most condescending look. If her door were closed, she would have banged her head on one of the few clear spaces on the surface of her great wooden desk. Since there were no corresponding emoticons that summed up her feelings, she simply typed, "Derrick. Come on..." and left him to figure it out. If he bothered to look up the term, he would realize that he was the poster-child for personality disorders, but she wasn't in the mood to instant message out a definition to him. Better to focus on the Rick Shaw "book." "Have u at least tried to make it funny?"

"As you so aptly put it, what would be the point of trying to make it funny if I have a personality disorder?" he countered.

"I don't know. B derivative. B quirky." Was she really saving any time by typing "B" instead of "Be"?

"I'll think about it," he typed back. "I have to go. I'm running out of time."

"Where are u?"

"Tokyo-Narita Airport. Pay computer. 100 yen for ten minutes." Since that was his last message, he must have run out of 100 yen coins.

Shirley closed out the IM session, checked her iPhone, and leaned back into her black leather chair that was incongruous with the rest of the décor but so comfortable that she didn't care. Most people found it difficult to hate Derrick. Actually liking him proved even more challenging, to be sure, but to actually hate him was difficult for most people to do. He offered up a lot of jarring, in-your-face honesty, which you at least had to respect, even though Shirley suspected that it was due as much to his social ineptitude as any sort of moral code. This complete aversion to bullshit would ruin any chance he had of working in the literary industry (and that included stocking shelves at a Barnes & Noble) once his writing career totally imploded, so at least Shirley had that advantage over him. It constituted one of the few advantages she could wrestle away from people like him, but thoughts like that kept her warm at night.

Unlike most people, Shirley could hate Derrick for a few very simple reasons. One involved envy. She tried to become an author, tried for twelve long years and had a big file folder stuffed with well over 100 tear-stained rejection letters to show for it. She moved to New York in the first place because the myopic, self-important publishers take you more seriously if your return address features a New York zip code. She uprooted her entire life and watched it crumble to pieces in a doomed attempt to become someone who mattered. Failing that, she scraped together the pieces and compromised with a career catering to the needs of individuals with more talent and/or luck than she could ever dream of.

Derrick, on the other hand, traveled a steep and linear path. He signed with a major publisher right after he could legally drink. And the fact that he couldn't repeat the feat means that the first time was pure luck, that he constituted the living embodiment of the metaphorical monkey chained to a typewriter. Still, he got the shot that she would have killed for... literally, *killed* for... stabbed someone with an ice pick in front of that someone's family for. Knowing that people like him existed somewhere in the world would have been hard enough for her to stomach, but since she legally represented the twit, he was now *her* monkey chained to a typewriter, and they both knew he wasn't cranking out another winner any time soon. Taking his calls, seeing his book on her bookshelf, browsing past his name on her email contact list... it was like having her own anti-trophy to mock her failures.

Shirley wanted to smoke, but even at midday, it was way too cold to stand outside for ten minutes, and the building's owner installed a smoke alarm in the ladies' restroom years ago (even though she thought the cigarettes always did a magnificent job of covering up the shit smell). Instead, she walked over and gently closed and locked her office door. Then, she marched back to the business side of her desk, unlocked her lower right desk drawer, pulled it open, and removed a bottle of Martel brandy that had remained sealed since her November birthday. She poured about an inch and a half into a used Starbucks cup she had drank from that morning. The combination of overly strong coffee residue and weak alcohol proved strangely tasty, not to the point where she would become like Samantha and replace coffee with alcohol as her work-related libation, but tasty like diner food at two in the morning. Shirley's enjoyment was short-lived, though; she was an angry drunk, and the booze wouldn't help her forget the fact that Derrick was ruining her life with his shitty writing. She had a client meeting at 4 p.m., leaving her just enough time to how on the computer and see how many Sylvia's lived in Peoria, Illinois.

*   *   *

CHAPTER FIVE:

THE GHOST OF SYLVIA SARSGAARD

About two years ago, Shirley had insisted that Derrick start a Facebook page. "It'll help you sell books," she had said, and even instructed her man-child assistant, Kenny, include a link on Derrick's Facebook page so that people could buy the books directly from the publisher and he would get a higher percentage of the sale. Derrick went along with the plan because Shirley seemed to know what she was talking about, but he drew the line at a Twitter account; he didn't want most people from his past to be able to find him at all, let alone track his daily activity at the push of a button. As for potential readers, the details of his daily life would probably repel twice as many people as they attracted.

Derrick checked the Facebook page every once in a while, usually when he had absolutely nothing to do, like at that precise moment in the Tokyo-Narita Airport. Generally, he alternated between thinking it was stupid waste of time and actively hating it. He didn't know how many books the page was responsible for selling and had no way of finding out (although he would guess it was a small number... a small, very round number), and he constantly received annoying friend-requests from people with whom he graduated high school. Even though he never even liked most of those people when he lived next door to them… not really… turning down friend-requests always bothered him. It felt rude, somehow, even though it shouldn't have, and even though he thought most of the requesters were idiots. So, he accepted the requests anyway. He would immediately regret it, but that wouldn't stop him the next time a friend request showed up in his email inbox. After all, idiots buy books, too, they just don't read them (except for the strange exception of *Atlas Shrugged*).

Beyond this purely monetary motivation, though, what the hell did he and his former classmates have to correspond about? "Bought a new truck. LOL!!!" Most of the people he'd grown up with led lives similar to one another… similar to the lives of their parents… and no matter how mundane the details of their lives, they still had made themselves a part of something. Derrick's life just wasn't like that, for good or ill. He still updated his page now and then, though, with book-related happenings, and he still checked it whenever he got stuck in airport/train station limbo. It was just maintenance; nothing interesting or enjoyable.

Derrick didn't mind airports nearly as much as airplanes because at least he could walk around (even though his spine had to endure the trauma from lugging his duffle bag around at all times as a function of his inability to trust his scant belongings to the high-school-dropouts who chuck bags for a living). The cookie-cutter uniformity of airports disturbed him to the point where they felt like parallel universes, but even they had distinct differences… a restaurant here or a statue there… that provided more variety than airplanes, and as Brian Austin Green once said, "Diversity keeps the flow hype." Some airports even had distinct personalities, even if those personalities were negative. The compartmentalized terminals of LAX reminded a stranded occupant of the different levels of hell. O'Hare was just a series of parallel corridors with nowhere to sit. Comparatively, a layover in Minneapolis felt like staying at the Ritz: numerous restaurants, secluded seating areas, and even one national landmark in the form of the men's restroom where Idaho Senator Larry Craig solicited a cop for gay sex. It's only real downside was the constant threat of a weather delay during six months of the year.

Tokyo's international airport disappointed Derrick. He'd visited Japan once before a couple years ago, and he went *through* Narita during that trip on his way to Kyoto, but the layover failed to make an impression on him. After watching *Lost in Translation*, he expected Tokyo to be a magical city… and maybe it was, but the airport sure as hell didn't provide anything special. He expected Zen gardens and pachinko parlors, maybe a geisha or two. Instead, there were barely even any restaurants, and a legion of duty-free shops consumed most of the free corridor space. There were several internet kiosks sprinkled about, but they cost about twelve cents per minute to use. Unfortunately, he had four hours to kill, a morphine hangover, and writer's block, so he started pumping 100 yen coins into the computer's money slot like it was primed to gush a jackpot.

Facebook didn't have much going on. Someone claiming to be a fan wanted to be "friends." So did a former classmate. *They should really come up with a better term for it than "friends,"* he mused. *"Acquaintances" and "contacts" sounds too formal, so they'd probably have to invent their own term, like how Twitter messages became "tweets."* Facials? Bookies? He didn't know. He accepted both friend requests. "Idiots buy books, too," he muttered to himself, like a cynic's mantra.

Another former classmate who had previously "friended" him now invited him to play an online game where one pretends to be a

Mafioso. *How does that even work? Did you get to fire at targets, or was it the adventure game equivalent of fantasy football?* Another invited him to join a group called "Fire Nancy Pelosi." *Oh, Person-I-Barely-Remember,* he thought, whimsically, *you know me just as well today as you did thirteen years ago.* He declined both offers.

With six minutes remaining on his 100-yen-coin, he surfed on over to Google and searched for the name "Rick Shaw." He actually got a couple hits for real people, but neither of them were the volleyball guy Shirley mentioned. One lived in Bowling Green, KY, and one lived in Ham Lake, MN, but other than the names of the towns they lived in, nothing funny or interesting appeared. He still might attempt to contact them, just to see if they had any amusing anecdotes about having that name... assuming that wouldn't open him up to a libel suit. In red letters at the top of the screen, Google made a suggestion: "Do you mean *rickshaw?*"

Despite most of his functioning brain knowing better, he typed the name "Sylvia Sarsgaard" into the text bar. He got the same information he did when he searched her name almost a year earlier, which either meant that she was living one boring-ass life or wasn't using that last name anymore, which probably meant that she was married. *Well,* he reflexively told himself, *I hope she's happy, wherever she is.* Part of him actually meant it, but that wasn't always the case. In years past, there were times when he overcame 3 a.m. bouts of insomnia by picturing himself smashing her beautiful smile with a frying pan, knocking out every single fucking one of her artificially whitened teeth. He had no idea why it helped him sleep; logically, fantasizing about violence seemed like it would crank up his sympathetic nervous system, but help it did. While not proud of those moments, he found the process strangely soothing, cathartic perhaps. Those days were (mostly) gone, and whether due to a lack of sleep problems or greater maturity, he was a better man for it.

He leaned back in the flexible, hard-plastic chair chained to the kiosk and watched the green numbers in the upper left-hand corner of the screen announcing that his session was timing out in less than sixty seconds. Why the fuck did Shirley have to bring up Sylvia? As if the morphine-induced stomachache and brain fog weren't enough of a bummer…Besides being unproductively shitty, Shirley knows how badly the topic bothers him; he wrote about a thinly-veiled parallel of their relationship in *Ham-Handed.* In the book, he made Sylvia out to be a real caste-iron bitch, but that was mainly for dramatic effect, to make the "Derrick" character a little more sympathetic (of course, then the trick became to not make the "Derrick" character look like a moron for having fallen for such a caste-iron bitch in the first place). His real feelings were far more complex.

Sylvia will remain forever distinct for having found him acceptable during the high-point of his existence, when he almost found himself acceptable. While that doesn't sound like a qualification for sainthood, so few people found him acceptable during any point in his life that one had to give credit where credit was due. They both entered college at the same time but didn't meet until their sophomore years, and while he wasn't the sort of person who wore black, ribbed, mock-turtleneck sweaters, sat in coffee shops, used words like "pseudointellectual," and talked about all the books he was going to write, she was. She held a central position in what he derisively referred to as The Literary Social Club, and even at the time, he really hated those people… *physically* hated them… probably more than was healthy, but she was hot, and for the young and perpetually celibate male, hotness trumps ideology surprisingly often.

Without Sylvia, he never would have endured a single poetry slam. With her, he subjected himself to five… five! She ran with a crowd that featured people with names like "Tristan" and "Cedric," like the cast of a Tennyson poem, and she rose to that most rarified air of the Literary Social Club by the easiest conceivable means: by being a bad poet. To be clear, Derrick believed that it took as much skill and effort to become a good poet as it took to become a good novelist, but it took infinitely less skill and effort to become a bad poet than a comparably bad novelist. The difference came down to volume. To become a bad novelist, one still has to produce a (bad) novel; that's a few hundred pages of shit. A bad poet, on the other hand, merely needs to produce a bad poem, and any idiot with a Doors album can scrawl a limerick on a cocktail napkin during a cross-campus bus ride.

Anyway, when *Dead Man in Sheets* got published and sold relatively well, he became a minor celebrity on campus, about on par with the football team's third-string quarterback; he made it into the school paper a few times, the local paper once, and was asked to give talks in English classes he'd been enrolled in a few months earlier. To those pasty freaks down at the coffee shop, though, he was bigger than Robert fucking Redford, because it wasn't like he published some science fiction novel about an intergalactic spice war in the Horsehead Nebula; it was an honest to gosh work of Literature, with generally positive reviews and everything. Derrick could mostly care less; compliments always made him uncomfortable because he always expected a "but" or a request to follow. He was far from immune to Sylvia's charms, though, and for her part, she got a little moist when he told her that the publisher planned to send him on a twelve-city book tour.

It went on like that for a while, two people using each other to impress people whose opinions didn't matter, but when he sent *Thanatos* to the publisher and they reflexively released it to capitalize on the positive momentum of *Dead Man*, it floundered and the clock on his proverbial fifteen minutes of fame started ticking. Derrick always felt bad about *Thanatos*. With a little more time and a little more work, he might have had a solid, respectable sophomore effort, but now it had been borne into the world, warts and all, and he couldn't ask for a do-over. He also felt bad when Sylvia broke up with him soon after *Thanatos* came out, less because he missed her and more because he missed the way she made him feel. For a little over a year, he felt loved and worthy of living in society with the "normal" people (in the most positive sense of the word). When she left, it confirmed all his worst fears about himself: he really was a disgusting person, and he didn't have quite enough talent to make his disgustingness not matter, to turn from a "weirdo" into an "eccentric." Time passed, and he came to the conclusion that he wasn't a bad person so much as bad at being a person, which is a little better. At the time, though, the sucking emptiness gnawing at his innards distracted him from such insight.

The hurt lingered for a long time, until three years ago, when he went to a mutual friend's wedding and saw her there. She looked good, but in an "alternate reality" kind of way. She had a tan, short hair, a push-up bra, and a boyfriend named "Chad." Chad was a banker with a thousand-watt smile who compulsively made eye contact when he spoke to you. In other words, he was exactly the sort of person who, had she encountered him in college, would have made her roll her eyes for effect and say something like, "God, look at that jackass." Derrick hated him even before he had to endure Chad's tight-grip, single-pump handshake that he and his frat brother probably worked on for hours on end. In a strange way, though, Chad's presence allowed Derrick to forgive Sylvia and get over her. She wasn't a strong person who rejected him because he was imperfect and didn't measure up to her; she was a weak, confused person who needed someone who she perceived as perfect and strong to latch onto, and it could have been Derrick, Chad, or Reinhard Heydrich for all she cared. It didn't mean that Derrick didn't have personality problems; it just meant that his personality problems were a separate issue.

Dredging up those memories of Sylvia and all that terrible poetry now made Derrick thirsty for a large black coffee, but not for that patchouli stench her former friends radiated. Fortunately for him, the Tokyo-Narita Airport contained a Starbucks. Unfortunately, it sat on the other side of the security checkpoint, and Derrick already felt lucky to have escorted his "prescription" medication through the first time. He'd have to drag his ass back toward the Italian-sounding café by Gate 26 and settle for an Americano (ugh) and half a Vicodin (yay!).

He shouldered his blue, canvas duffle bag and winced through the neck pain as he scanned the directory situated next to the trash can. A little over two hours remained before his flight even started to pre-board, so he might as well fully examine his options on his quest to find the least repellent cup of coffee in Terminal 1. His thoughts were scattered, so much so that he had to read the directory a second time. He would have shaken his head if his neck didn't ache so badly. *Why the fuck did Shirley bring up Sylvia?*

*   *   *

CHAPTER SIX:

SMALL DOGS

Shirley fired up a Parliament Light as she trudged up the steps from the subway station, toward the waning daylight. She wore functional dress shoes with a broad, two-inch heel, which helped her maintain balance on the wet concrete. As soon as the end of the cigarette started burning, a gust of wind slammed into her with the force of blitzing linebacker. If her lips hadn't reflexively clamped around the filter, she might have lost an eye. If her gloved hand hadn't flailed out and grasped the railing, she might have landed on the thirty-something Mexican woman trying to ease her baby stroller down the steps. It was going to be another dank, East Coast Spring day.

She took the final step to street level, and chief among the assorted thoughts twirling around in her head was *why the fuck did I bring up the girlfriend with Derrick?* It struck her as way too obvious an attempt to manipulate his emotions, and that shit happened almost ten years go. *Obviously, he's learned to cope with it*, she told herself as she stalked down the block with the top of crown of her skull cutting through the wind, *after ten years, he wouldn't be alive right now if he hadn't learned to cope with it.* She tried to hit him with a sucker punch to the gut, and if it came off as overly petty, he might stop listening to her.

She had no idea whether she could actually pull this off, but she certainly didn't underestimate the complexity of the human heart. How exactly does one convince another to shuffle off his or her (in this case, his) mortal coil? Cult leaders probably do it all the time, but how many real people have even tried? People off themselves on a daily basis with no coaxing, but how many actually have to *resist* coaxing? She turned past the vegetable stand on the corner and glanced through squinted eyes and a slight drizzle down the block to the stoop of her brownstone poking into the sidewalk. In two minutes, she could be opening her front door and walking into the warm, dry, wind-resistant embrace of her apartment, but if answers to her dilemma awaited her anywhere, they lurked in the opposite direction. She lifted one of her Isotoners to her mouth and gave a cough that sounded like a garbage disposal grinding up a broccoli stalk, shouldered her purse, and slogged onward in the direction of Prospect Park.

*   *   *

Karen stuck her face into the space offered by the front door's security chain. She was a handsome woman from this angle, when you couldn't see the hairdo that looked like the molded coiffure of a plastic action figure. "Shirley?" Karen said in her perpetually smug tone. Half the time, she didn't even mean to do it; she was the only person Shirley knew who could sound like a bitch saying, *I'm sorry to hear about your dad dying,* but there you have it. Two rat-sized dogs jumped up and down and barked behind Karen as she slid the security chain off the door. Shirley hated those dogs. Their unnerving thinness and stretched faces made them look like zombie dogs, and the scarce patches of hair didn't help, either. She didn't even know what kind of dog they were; identifying dog breeds was never her specialty. She knew what a Golden Retriever looked like, though, and in her mind, the further a creature deviated from that image, the less dog-like it became. These things looked like they'd lived in the intestinal tract of a Golden Retriever, then ate its remains after it died. "I assume you're not dropping me as a client, because we both know you'd do that over the phone," Karen said as Shirley walked past, the dogs taking turns pawing at Shirley's pant-legs.

Shirley ignored the dogs as she hung her wet overcoat on the coatrack by the door; in a warm, dry apartment, their behavior was tolerable. "Of course not," Shirley chided, neglecting to add, *Where else could I find someone to write murder mysteries for women 35 to 60?* Even if she had, Karen probably wouldn't have taken offense; her eyes showed the telltale reddish tinge of a recent baking session, and the thick, Lavender & Vanilla mist of Glade hanging in the air didn't exactly refute that hypothesis. "I'm not interrupting anything, am I?" she asked, easing down onto the couch cushion nearest the door.

"Oh, of course not," Karen assured her, flapping an arm languidly and laughing to herself in a manner that gloriously confirmed Shirley's suspicion. *Thank god it's weed,* she thought, *Karen's a terrible…* terrible *drunk.* Not that she was judging. On the contrary, she had a difficult time relating to people who didn't get fucked up on *something* on a regular basis. Life was a fucking grind, and as John Lennon would say, whatever gets you through the night, baby, it's all right. "My bastard of an ex-husband took the kids for an extended weekend to Hershey Park, wherever the fuck that is," she looked down at the yapping mutts pogoing around the white carpet as if Shirley was the first human they'd ever seen, "but at least he left me with my babies." Her eyes widened. "Scotty. Get down! Not on the couch! You know better than that."

Shirley hoped that if she remained still, the dogs would cease to notice her, but maybe that rule only applied to snakes. "Bastard of an ex-husband" was an extraordinarily trite expression, and she seriously doubted that Lars would have taken those dogs any further than the Humane Society if he had the option, but Shirley didn't call out Karen on either point. Instead, she quietly anticipated Karen making a joke about how, if the kids wanted to ride a rollercoaster, Lars could have just bought them a token for the A Train. *Wait for it... Wait for it... Eh, screw it.* "Why drive all the way to Pennsylvania when all you have to do is buy them a ticket on the A Train?" Shirley asked.

Karen frowned. "Pennsylvania? What about it?"

"That's where Hershey Park is."

"No shit," Karen said in her smoky monotone. She sat down on her off-white easy chair that matched the couch and curled her thick legs up under her. On a clear day, the sun came through the diaphanous curtains, and that spot in front of the window became luminous, but it was far from a sunny day. "Is it chocolate-themed?"

"Not so much," Shirley replied from Karen's off-white couch (smokers don't get to have white furniture... not for long, anyway). It also didn't help the aesthetic that greasy strands of dog hair poked out of every crease in the upholstery. Why would someone have white furniture and two rust-colored dogs? She contemplated that and continued to gently push dogs off of her black pant-legs. Shirley never cared for dogs, even Golden Retrievers; as a species, they were essentially well-meaning idiots. Yes, most experts insist that dogs are smarter than cats, but what does that really mean? There's more to intelligence than memory. She especially hated small dogs: they had all the annoying tendencies of large dogs, but shrunken down to useless proportions. Karen's two little rodents wouldn't have been able to deter a midget thief. At least their rate of yapping had slowed down after they realized that Shirley wasn't going to kill them or feed them.

"Thank god. I was picturing something like those old commercials for the Land of Dairy Queen." Karen's wispy eyebrows bobbed. "I almost sent Scarlet with her floaties, just in case Lars took her to the river of fudge."

"It would have to be molten fudge," Shirley pointed out and took her eyes off the dogs long enough to receive a perplexed look from Karen. "You know, to keep it from turning back into a solid."

Karen snickered drunkenly. "Well, someone earned her 'A' in Chemistry."

Shirley smiled her tight-lipped smile that constituted more of a refusal to open her mouth out of fear of speaking than an actual smile. It was always difficult to be the lone sober person in the room, even when the room only contained one other person. It almost felt like traveling through the Uncanny Valley; everything was a little... off. "It's too long since we got together like this," Shirley said when she finally trusted herself to speak. The dogs had moved on to running in idiot figure-eights on the rug and barking intermittently. Karen seemed to have acclimated to the shrill little sounds emanating from their sharp little maws long ago, like parents who ignore their crying infant on airplanes, much to the chagrin of everyone around them. Either that or she was stoned even worse than Shirley thought.

"Yeah," Karen emphatically agreed, "so why don't you tell me what prompted it?" Shirley tried to look surprised or hurt, but before her eyes could widen too far, she could inhale too much, or her hand could find her sternum, Karen waved it all away. "Oh please, girl; you aren't the pop-in type, especially for social things. You always have your Excel calendar put together a month in advance. So, as the British say, out with it, then."

"I'm writing again," Shirley said, reflexively, even though she didn't expect that particular lie to come out. It wasn't a good lie, not because it was obviously bullshit, but because it took the mood to a bad place. She hated condescension, and when she lobbed that one up to a professional writer who'd played the game as long as Karen… well, she kind of asked for it. Shirley originally had planned to ease into a conversation and subtly try to steer it toward darker themes and wait for someone to mention topics peripherally related to major depression or suicide. Karen's drug-induced bluntness foiled that plan. "I'm trying to get one of my characters to get another character to commit suicide, and I don't know how."

Karen gave her a long, uncritical look, then abruptly said, "I'm thirsty. Would you care for a glass of water?" She unfolded her legs and rose from the couch in one fluid motion.

"Uh, no," Shirley said. "No thanks." Her eyes followed Karen into the kitchen, along with the pair of dogs twirling in their owner's wake, and for a second, she thought Karen might call the cops. The possibility made her mouth dry, even though the logical part of her brain knew the criminal code well enough to remind her that she had nothing to worry about. When Karen started to pour the Brita water into a glass, Shirley called into the kitchen, "On second thought, I would like a glass of water."

"On the rocks?" Karen called out.

"No, just wet is fine."

A few long seconds passed, filled with panting and the clink of glassware. "One of the things I miss about Scarlett being a baby was that we always had a lot of PediaLyte in the house," Karen said, returning with two tumblers of water and setting them both on a pair of cork coasters that sat on top of her glass coffee table. "But, that's why God created water." Mercifully, the dogs had moved on to molesting one another on the kitchen tile. "So, that's the entire plot?" Karen said, her eyes catching Shirley again though a thin curtain of light brown bangs.

"No, that's not the *whole* plot, but that's the part I'm stuck on," Shirley said, then took a long drink of her water. *That's still better than Derrick's idea,* she thought with some satisfaction. *All he has is a name.* No one would ever describe Derrick as a creative dynamo; he was just weird. For instance, one of Derrick's characters liked to ask to use other people's bathrooms so that he could rummage through the medicine cabinets and steal prescription medication. She assumed that Derrick did that in real life, so it couldn't be considered creative, could it? Maybe in terms of stealing drugs, but not in terms of writing, right?

Karen sat back down and crossed the right leg of her beige slacks over her left, clearly sharpening as the conversation evolved. The slacks clashed with the upholstery. "Did you ever see *The Tenant?*"

"No. Should I have?"

"Yeah. It's good. Polanski. The '70's… back before the whole pedophile thing." Karen took two gulps from her water glass. "Well, what's the deal with the character you want to commit suicide?"

"Well, *I* don't want him to commit suicide," Shirley said, a bit defensively, then reminded herself that "making someone commit suicide" isn't against the law and regained her composure. "I don't even know how the situation is going to resolve itself. My main character wants him to do it so that he can inherit his money."

"What's the character like?" Karen asked. "The suicidal person."

Shirley thought about it. How to describe a real person in a sound bite? "He's the isolated, depressed sort," she said.

Karen's thin eyebrows bobbed. "Well thank god; half you're work's already done. Now, all you have to do is create a loss."

"Loss," Shirley repeated. "Loss of what?"

"Doesn't matter," Karen said with the assurance of an expert. "Loss of health. Loss of a relationship. Loss of a job. Cops in my books always look for a motive for murder, even if it's self-murder, and the reason for suicide is usually loss, even if it's the loss of hope. That's what 'sadness' is after all: an emotional reaction to loss. Haven't you read the *Book of Job*?"

"The Heinlein book?" Shirley loved Robert Heinlein. Reading *Stranger in a Strange Land* in high school made her want to write novels. Even though girls weren't supposed to like science fiction, it didn't matter to Shirley; girls weren't supposed to write, either, unless it was love letters to David Cassidy. Reading all that brilliant shit was such a joy as a kid, because she knew she could get better. She was just starting out as a writer, so reading a masterpiece gave her something to aspire to. As the years went by, though, it became harder to read a truly great book. She'd peaked as a writer, and she didn't have all the time in the world anymore, so if she happened upon a book that was truly great, it served as a monument to something she could never do.

"The original."

"Job didn't commit suicide," Shirley corrected, then wished she hadn't, because she realized that that wasn't the point.

"Of course he didn't commit suicide!" Karen said, a split second after Shirley's internal editor did the same. Karen leaned forward and playfully slapped at the air between them, clearly enjoying her dominant position in the discussion. "He felt despair, though, and that's because he lost everything, house, family, etcetera. But he *didn't* kill himself because he still had faith. If he'd lost that, it all would have been over, and the Devil would have won his bet with God."

"Yeah, I forgot there was a bet," Shirley said, slowly nodding. That detail of the story always struck her as unnervingly petty on God's part. It might have been a major plot point in the Heinlein book, too, but she couldn't remember the whole thing. How did it apply to Derrick? *What can you take away from someone who roams the earth like Caine in* Kung Fu? she wondered. "What if the person doesn't have anything?" she asked as Karen dug into the tinder box centered on her coffee table.

"Then you have a boring book," Karen said, smiling slyly with a fresh white joint trapped between her unnaturally bright red lips. "But seriously, all you have to do is give them something," she said, extending a red Bic lighter toward Shirley, then pulling it back, "then take it away." She lifted the lighter within six inches of her mouth and paused. "You don't care if I fire up, do you?"

*   *   *

CHAPTER SEVEN:

SEOUL SURVIVOR

"Unhand her, you fiend," Rick Shaw shouted at the villainous individual who held his alter ego's current love interest dangling over something far below and/ or potentially dangerous.

"I would be careful with my choice of words," the villain said. "Letting her go at this point would certainly prove fatal."

Rick froze at the precipice. The villain was right. Maybe if he was the Rascal or Helen Wheels, he might have been able to reach her before his enemy gave that fateful shove. If he was the Para-Sailor, the Sub-Dude, or Madame Zipline, he might have been able to catch her before she hit the spinning blades of the thresher. None of the Fellow Travelers were present, though; it was just him, Rick Shaw, with all the powers and limitations that involved. "All right, then," he said, holding his empty hands in front of him. He would opt for the diplomatic route... for now. "What do you want?"

"You know exactly what I want, Mr. Shaw," the villain (something having to do with roadkill... Road Killer... Head Pizza...) said and allowed Rick's imagination to run wild during the couple seconds of pregnant silence. "I want to see

you personally carry all of the gold from your Fort Knox and deliver it to me in front of a famous local landmark by Friday at midnight."

Rick Shaw's mouth fell open, and his tongue skimmed his lower lip. He badly wanted to tell the Road Killer to shove his demands into any available orifice, but the look on Linda's(?) face froze the breath in his lungs. He got her into this mess via something having to do with his double-life, and if anyone could shoulder the responsibility of getting her out again, it was Rick Shaw. Circumstances might have already destroyed their chance at a relationship, and that hurt, but not nearly as much as watching her get torn into a million pieces. "Just give me the directions," Rick said, still trying to sound defiant amid his capitulation, "and one way or another, I'll bring it there on time."

*   *   *

Derrick liked the international airport outside of Seoul much better than the one outside of Tokyo; it had not one, but two Dunkin' Doughnuts. He wasn't a big doughnut fiend, but their black coffee was hard to beat, especially in East Asia, where the only competitor was Starbucks. The smell of the freshly brewed cup of coffee alone went a long way to compensating for the fact that the outlet adaptor he bought in Tokyo didn't work in Korea. *Isn't Japan, like, ninety miles away?* he wondered as he stared at the power cord lying uselessly on the brown tile floor of the doughnut shop. The adaptors were also surprisingly hard to find. It was an *international* airport, after all; since Korea seemed to be the only country in the world with triangular, round, three-pronged outlets, shouldn't they sell adaptors in every retail shop in the airport? Shouldn't they offer you one when you go through Customs & Immigration? He managed to find a five-foot high, circular rack of them at an electronics store on the far side of security, but since the instructions were in Korean and the sales associate spoke Korean at him, he just had to assume he was purchasing the correct one and hope for the best.

"Gamsa hamnida," he said and performed a brief head nod to the perpetually smiling cashier. He pronounced it like the stewardesses on the flight from Tokyo: "gom-som-nida," as if it had four syllables. In the air above the Sea of Japan, he cracked open his English-to-Korean Dictionary and Phrase Book and learned how to say "hello," "bathroom," and "subway." Even when combined with "thank you" and "excuse me," it didn't constitute the most impressive linguistic arsenal in the world, but he hoped that that collection would provide the fertile soil from which an impressive phrase-garden would blossom. He undoubtedly would soon wish he'd learned more useful word combinations (like "please stop talking to me" or "I demand to speak with the United States embassy"), but languages were never Derrick's thing. Even after a month of language work, he would have a smaller vocabulary than one of those signing gorillas who people were always buying kittens for. Maybe that's why he liked writing so much: English and he were just as comfortable together as a pair of old shoes.

Aside from the game of adaptor roulette he was forced to play, another unpleasant surprise waiting for Derrick when he left the airport was that the airport sat almost two freakin' hours from downtown Seoul. That's like putting an airport to serve New York City in Philadelphia. Despite his brain-sucking cocktail of jet lag and sleep deprivation, Derrick braved the two hours of subway travel and three transfers necessary to reach his hotel. Not that he could complain too much: the maps were printed and the stops were announced in both Korean and English, and compared to taking public transportation in, say, Detroit, riding the subway in Seoul was like receiving a professional blowjob. It struck him as almost oppressively safe. The main problem he encountered on the journey had nothing to do with logistics; each passing moment required more and more effort to remain awake, and left him with less and less effort to give. At one point, he nodded off, only to awaken with a rush of panic, but a mere five minutes had passed, and he only missed one stop.

The subway didn't get too crowded, and the Koreans didn't seem to notice him, especially. There was no obvious pointing and laughing, at least. Half a dozen foreigners sat in various parts of the car, most white, one black. People in Seoul were probably used to the non-Asian faces, at least more so than people out in the nation's factory towns and industrial centers. This city hosted an Olympics over twenty years ago, for Christ's sake, and you don't get much more international than that.

At last, Derrick dragged his ass, his duffle bag, and his laptop case up the top steps of the Itaewon Subway Station. His ten-story hotel towered over him on the left, with the sun either rising or setting behind it. The neighborhood of Itaewon sat about half a mile from an American military base, so it was, roughly speaking, "the American section" of the city ("Ameritown," maybe, or "Americatown"). From the top of the subway steps, without turning his head, Derrick could see a Starbucks, a Burger King, and a Quiznos (which he wasn't sure still even existed in the U.S.). For the most part, hanging out in these sorts of sections of foreign cities never appealed to Derrick, since they were essentially inferior copies of the places he was coming from, but he *did* like being able to speak to and get understood by the hotel staff. Thus, he was in luck.

"Hello, Mr. Kessler," the comely lass at the front counter said as she looked at his passport and typed something into her desktop computer. "I see that you'll be staying with us for nine nights." She had a slight accent, but compared to a lot of places in the U.S. (think southern… deep southern), she might as well have spoken the Queen's English. Derrick smiled a genuine smile for the first time in a while. This was an awesome set-up for him: he could sleep here, surrounded by people who would understand him if he needed to order food or an ambulance, and when he wanted to explore the rest of the city, the subway entrance sat about fifty feet away from the hotel's front lobby.

Traveling to places in order to run marathons proved far more complex than Derrick would have ever fathomed before he started doing it. Running was such a simple behavior, after all. Part of the problem is that you can't really fly in one day and run the next because of the havoc airplane travel wreaks on your joints and the rest of your body, but if you go several days in advance, you can't do anything fun because if you walk too far or eat something your system isn't used to, you could end up with a debilitating case of diarrhea on race day. Some people have the physical advantage of possessing more resilient bodies, but Derrick wasn't one of those people. His advantage involved enough disposable time and income to afford him the luxury of arriving a few days before the race and a leaving a few days afterward. He could probably soak up a substantial hunk of Korean culture in about ten days, beyond even what his extensive viewing of *M*A*S*H* could provide. Then, it would be back to America for five months, with another temp job and another race to train for. He was thinking of giving Portland a shot (either Portland, OR, or Portland, ME), and he seriously considered sending in some applications for Master's of English programs in the fall. Not to suck his own dick, but with all his publication record, any program would be dying to take him. Then, in two short years, he could teach at colleges for his part-time work instead of work in factories or loading docks.

He unlocked the door to his hotel room using an old-fashioned metal key. Apparently, keycard technology hadn't reached South Korea yet. One feature of the room that did impress him was the slot on the wall where you had to shove the rod attached to your key in order for the power in the room to operate. That way, if you left the room (and had the wherewithal to take your key with you), you wouldn't be wasting juice.

He'd encountered this technology before in Japan and, after getting madly frustrated and almost breaking his ankle the first time, as he stomped around in the dark trying to figure out why the lights didn't work, he came to the conclusion that it just made good sense. He eased his luggage straps off his shoulders and set his duffle bag on the easy chair and his laptop on the desk. He also stepped over to the bed and pushed down on the mattress with his fingertips, finding it soft-ish. This was a relief: all of the travel guidebooks at Barnes & Noble he read without buying warned about the procrustean nature of Korean mattresses, and nothing could fuck up a twenty-six mile run worse than aching neck and back... except for his old nemesis: diarrhea.

A yellow cord stretched out of the wall underneath the window to indicate the internet connection. Derrick hooked it into his laptop and fired up the computer. It took a few minutes to surge to life, but when it did, a bubble at the bottom of the screen told him that he had a new message from Shirley. If he'd been seated at the desk when he saw it, he might have taken the time to read it. However, while waiting for the laptop to turn on, he had planted his ass on the mattress and removed his running shoes, which meant that he merely had to lie back and he would be asleep in ten seconds.

And that's what he did. And that's what he was.

*   *   *

When Derrick awakened two and a half hours later, he immediately slogged across the room to his computer. The screensaver image gracing his laptop was of a young woman sitting on the beach, smiling broadly at the camera. He used to know her: they internet dated for a little over three weeks. He never met her in person, but she sent him pictures a few days into their "relationship." She was beautiful, with long, reddish brown hair and longer legs, and he had once heard...

somewhere… that women don't want handsome men, they want men
who can get beautiful women. So, he put the photos on his screensaver,
and when anybody asked him about them, he told them that she was an
ex-girlfriend but that he didn't want to talk about it. Looking at one of
the smiling images now (this one featured her standing on a pier
overlooking an anonymous body of water, wearing sunglasses), he decided
that she would find it distinctly unnerving that he used those pictures for
that purpose, and it would provide her little solace that Derrick's strategy
had failed miserably. The photos had remained in place for three years,
because during that time, he never received any pictures from flesh-and-
blood women to replace the ones from his internet flame.

With a few waves of his fingers, he made the photos evaporate
and clicked on the link to the email message. The message read:

Derrick:

*Unbelievable news!! Nothing is set in stone, yet, but I may have found a publisher for
"Re-Ality." We're talking about a big house and an almost six-figure advance!!
Again, I'm still working out the details, but I'll update you as soon as I find out
anything new. This is it, man! Your break into the BIG time!*

Yours,

Shirley

Derrick stared at the screen for a long time… so long that he had
to wave his fingers again to keep the screen saver from coming back to
life. After first, he thought he was in shock; the emotional weight of not
having made a step forward in ten years finally evaporating and him not
being prepared for it. It's objectively hard to tell if you're in shock,
though. So, he read it again. After several minutes of not moving except
to breathe and blink, he finally realized that he simply didn't believe it (not

"I don't believe it!" but "I don't believe it... full-stop"). He read over the message from beginning to end a third time, and several discordant elements jumped out at him.

Issue Number One: To be totally honest, he never really liked *Re-Ality*, his most recent literary masterpiece. On one hand, a book was subjectively like a child he bore into the world, and like any parent not in danger of having his children taken from him by the state, he was proud of it and loved it on some level, but like any parent of a child older than two, he could attain some level of objectivity and recognize strengths and weaknesses when they appeared. So many weaknesses... Like any book, he really thought it was some life-altering shit while he was vomiting it out onto the page. Objectivity usually arrived about two weeks after the completion of the fourth draft, and objectively, he found the plot predictable, the dialogue preachy, and the characters transparently recycled version of characters from previous books. Plus, he hated the title; it was a working title he never got around to updating.

On the other hand, he'd heard... somewhere... that writer's aren't the best judge of their own work. For the record, he considered that idea complete bullshit, but that's what he heard.

Issue Number Two: Related to Issue Number One, even if *Re-Ality* got picked up by some publisher desperate for a "name" writer, it couldn't *possibly* be worth a six-figure advance. It was barely worth the cost of supersizing his extra value meal. He could crank out something comparable *right now* if someone gave him one week and a couple gallons of hot coffee.

On the other hand, he wasn't terribly familiar with Shirley's negotiating strategy. Maybe she used "six figures" as her initial offer and anticipated that it would come down after they made a counter offer. If that was true, though, why mention that amount to him? He might do something stupid, like make a down payment on a house (well, okay, not that *specific* stupid thing but something equally stupid that didn't involve the illusions of permanence that Derrick shunned).

Issue Number Three (and most disturbing of all): What was with all the exclamation points? There were five exclamation points in that email! Had Shirley gotten possessed by a thirteen-year-old who just won a radio call-in contest? Modern nomads lead a surprisingly fastidious existence, and Derrick had managed to save every email he ever received from Shirley… for potential litigation purposes, not sentimentality. The count had ballooned to something in the neighborhood of 300 messages, and if he were to go back through all of them, he doubted that he would be able to find five exclamation points. It wouldn't have surprised him to learn that her computer didn't come with that key. Beyond that, he would easily bet $5,000 that she never called him "man."

On the other hand, Shirley was supposedly in trouble at the agency and needed a submission to hit, so maybe she was worked up and happy for herself and/or him, which was fine. Maybe she was *really* happy and did a few lines of cocaine to celebrate. In fact, if this whole… whatever it was… was real, Derrick would select recreational drug use as the most probable explanation for all the exclamation.

In any case, he didn't actually believe that Shirley had found a buyer willing to pay $100,000 for arguably his worst book, but because he knew that chronically depressed individuals tended to emotionally undercut their own success, he decided to maintain his trademark cautious optimism. If it happened, great. If it didn't, something good would probably come out of it, right? Now, the only thing he really had left to worry about was his reflexive *planning*.

Derrick lacked the ability to read people. Body language, tone of voice, choice of terms… he deciphered these social cues like an autistic three-year-old. An unfortunate consequence of this was that when he did receive a solid piece of concrete evidence about something, within minutes, he started generating elaborate scenarios around this kernel of truth. Meeting a woman for the first time and finding out that "she likes my book" quickly metastasizes into "I wonder if her religious beliefs will become an issue when deciding what school we will send our kids to." On a flight, "we are experiencing turbulence" becomes "I wonder how long I'll be able to tread water in the North Atlantic." So, despite being fully aware of this tendency, despite warning himself against it, it didn't take long after reading Shirley's email for him to coordinate the book tour with the talk show circuit, at least in his head.

With these images involuntarily dancing in his head, Derrick walked out of the hotel a little after dawn to find some breakfast. He strolled along on a cushion of air that had nothing to do with space-age technology of his New Balance shoes. Even though he was trying to keep his diet (and by extension, his bowl movements) consistent, he decided to indulge himself with a Crissandwich from the Itaewon Burger King. Even in a country that didn't appreciate breakfast, one could always count on the King. After that, it was off to take an early morning constitutional and form broad stereotypes of people living in South Korea.

One of the first cultural spectacles to greet him on his walk was the cross-traffic refusing to yield for a fire truck and an ambulance. As he turned away from this, thinking about how such blind self-interest represented an uber-capitalist's wet dream, he came within inches of getting impaled by the handlebar of a motorcycle as it sputtered down the sidewalk at close to twenty-five miles per hour. He actually heard its approach seconds before, but he didn't anticipate it actually cruising down the freakin' *sidewalk*. Three middle aged guys, squatting on their haunches, drinking alcohol out of green bottles chuckled in his direction. "Jesus

Christ," Derrick muttered as the motorcycle, which was apparently delivering friend chicken, shortly after dawn, sped away. "I'm going to be lucky to survive until the marathon."

He attempted to keep exploring the immediate environs, but his brain still felt like it was operating at half-speed, so his heart really wasn't up to the task. He headed back to the room and tried to go to back to sleep, but whether due to jet lag or exhilaration, it didn't work. He just lay in bed with his eyes closed for an hour, until he gave up and flipped through the TV channels for a few minutes. When that failed to stimulate him, he returned to the warm embrace of the Internet.

A couple years ago, Derrick took a six-day trip to Kyoto, Japan (which proved far more expensive than a ten-day trip to Korea), and he'd actually been under the impression that Korea was fairly similar to Japan since people looked the same, bowed a lot, couldn't pronounce the letter "L," and excelled at the same Olympic sports. During his brief time in the South Korea, however, he had already discovered several distinct differences between the populations:

1) Japan has much cleaner air, personal hygiene, and just about everything else.
2) Japanese eat raw fish. Koreans eat fermented cabbage and radishes, which also plays into the previous point. They both eat approximately equal amounts of rice.
3) Japan has two sports worth watching: baseball and sumo wrestling. Korea only has baseball, and since it was early March, Derrick was shit out of luck on that front.
4) Japanese value personal space a lot more than Koreans. By the end of that first day, he would see more women holding hands and men with their arms around each other than at a gay pride

parade… yet, according to the internets, homosexuality is illegal in Korea. Maybe the behavioral leap is too short to acknowledge.

5) (Related to number 4) Koreans are a lot pushier. Deplaning in Tokyo and deplaning in Seoul were about as different as participating in a march and participating in a riot. People in Seoul spilled into the aisles like the plane was on fire.

Looking at the tourist sites on the web, Derrick wondered what the fuck he was going to do for the week-plus in Korea, besides visit Buddhist temples. He *could* go visit the DMZ, which Bill Clinton once called "the Most Dangerous Place in the World" and MSN.com included in their list of World Tourist Attractions to Avoid, but somehow that seemed like a direct "fuck you" to Bill Clinton and MSN. The world's largest department store failed to entice him, especially since it resided on the opposite side of the peninsula in Busan. Maybe they had a particularly tall building he could visit or a particularly fast train he could ride.

Damn you, M*A*S*H, he thought, drumming his fingers on the top of the almost burgundy wooden desk, *I could have been running in Denmark.*

*   *   *

CHAPTER EIGHT:

SHOVELING ON THE LIES

Derrick's email reply struck Shirley as a little too cautiously optimistic. She wasn't certain, because his email messages always sounded so stilted, but he barely even mentioned the "good news" and instead started yammering about trying to use Rick Shaw as one of several vehicle-themed super-heroes. It sounded more like the idea for a Saturday morning cartoon than the basis of a novel, but to be fair, it wasn't a terrible idea for a cartoon. At least it was a big step up from his attempt at writing a romance novel; Derrick probably understood the minds of children better than he understood the minds of women.

Shirley clearly needed to up the ante, to kindle a flicker of optimism, and although multiplying the lies threatened to make her motivations too glaringly obvious, the threat of an imminent firing loomed over her and demanded that she take some chances. She waited until the end of the work day, then sent off another email. With the time change, he wouldn't be able to read the message until the next morning, which was nature's way of helping her space out her lies.

Derrick:

Just got off the phone with a producer. There's been a lot of buzz with the situation with "Re-Ality," and a studio wants to do a "Dead Man" movie. There's virtually nothing in the way of details so far, but I'll keep you posted as things develop. A word of warning: I've been down this road a couple times before and it never panned out, but maybe the third time's a charm!

Yours,

Shirley

She hit send, knowing that it was the last card she could play for the near future. For some writers, you could try to entice them by throwing some ambiguous "award buzz" into the mix, but not for Derrick. Granted, increasing his status as a minor celebrity would threaten to give him some kind of social life, but subjective accolades always made Derrick feel guilty, like he didn't deserve it. Conversely, the movie thing was gold: nothing got his attention like a chance at surefire, long-term income. It wasn't that he was greedy; he lived life like a pauper who chanced upon a trash bag full of aluminum cans that morning, but he liked to travel and he hated normal jobs, and if you're that unreliable, you've got to find stability somewhere.

Certainly, she could keep piling on the "maybes," but if she strung these two possibilities along for a while, pumping up his hope a little more and a little more every day, he'd start to make rationalizations like, "well, even if I don't get them both, as long as I get one, my life's going to get a little better." Then, after he got comfortable and a little satisfied with his projected lot in life, she could drop the bomb, telling him he wasn't getting either and that she was firing him as a client because he was a gigantic failure. That would really deliver the ol' stomach punch.

Shirley sunk her shoulders into her high-backed, leather office chair and pursed her lips, thoughtfully. Now, if she could just take away his supply of pharmaceuticals and find a way to break his leg so he couldn't run so damned much, he'd really spiral out of control.

A voice in her head reflexively reminded Shirley that wishing harm on someone else invoked bad karma, but that voice had stayed silent for so long that it sounded laughably soft. She wasn't the superstitious sort. In her experience, people seldom got what they deserved: most got less and a few got way more than they deserved. Hard work only mattered when you combined it with a shitload of luck. Plus, if she was wrong and they did live in a fair, well-ordered universe, Derrick had already built up enough positive karma over his fortunate little life; all she was really asking for was to sponge up enough of it for herself to keep her fucking job that she didn't especially like. Besides, she wasn't *killing* him. She wasn't even directly making his life worse. All she was doing was creating a situation that would increase the chances of him perceiving his life as utterly worthless, to the point where he *might* entertain the idea of taking his own life. Whether he actually acted on the idea was his decision...

Someone gently knocked on her door, breaking Shirley out of the spell she was in. "Oh, hey Luis," she said to the green suited janitor. "Enough wind out there for you today?"

"Hello, Mees," Luis said. "I'm here for the trash." That's what Luis said every day, no matter what she said to him. Shirley wasn't convinced that that was the extent of his English proficiency, but other than inserting "meester" in place of "mees" when the occasion warranted, that was all he seemed willing to impart. *Good for him*, she thought as he pushed the door the rest of the way open and shuffled into her office. *Small talk is overrated.* At home, he probably bitched about the lazy, white (and Asian… and black) dumbasses he picked up trash for, and he probably did it with the voice of a character is *Masterpiece Theatre.*

Luis picked up the dented aluminum trashcan by the door and pounded on the bottom to drop the contents into his Rubbermaid trashcan on wheels. He did it every day, but Shirley actually watched him this time. Even if he did know more English than he let on, Luis wasn't the sort of guy who would try to convince someone to commit suicide. He was a simple man, a family man (probably).

"Do you have a family, Luis?" Shirley asked.

Luis nodded, but it probably served more as a reaction to vocally generated sound than a reaction to content. "Thank you, Mees," he said, backing out the door.

Salt of the earth, that one. What would he do, though, to keep his trash can emptying job? Shirley had to wonder. What if losing that job meant that Luis's (hypothetical) family would starve? He would probably lie, cheat, steal, and otherwise do whatever he had to do to survive. And while Shirley had no family to speak of, that also meant that there would be no one to care for her in her approaching golden years. Only Shirley looked out for Shirley, so Shirley had better stop morally equating herself to simple-minded janitors.

After Luis stepped out of her office and gently pulled the door closed behind him, she descended into thought again. Maybe she could tip off the South Korean authorities that Derrick had a couple bottles of prescription dope on his person. They didn't take kindly to narcotics trafficking in the land of kim chee (*Kim Chee*… maybe she could date Rick Shaw). Even if he didn't off himself, his life turning into *Midnight Express* would be good press.

Knowing Derrick, though, he'd probably manage to screw up a drug possession charge, too… somehow. Despite all the breaks he'd gotten, he'd never built anything out of his life, never made himself a part of something. He just turned into some loner who bounced along on this perpetual wave of mediocrity. Hell, if Shirley could get him to off himself, she might be doing him a *favor.* At his current rate, he'd die an older, lonely marginally successful writer. Wouldn't it be better to die relatively young, with all the world still wondering, "What if?" Samantha was right: when we look back, all we remember about Jim Morrison is that he was sex in leather pants because we never got to see him as a bloated, old has-been, who either transformed into something unrecognizable (a slightly darker David Crosby) or a pathetic shadow of his former self still trying to fit into those leather pants.

With any luck at all, she could drop a few more hints of success for Derrick, and his habit of compulsively planning would do her work for her before she pulled the rug out. Derrick tended to construct a certainty from a vague notion; a few times in the past, she mentioned a possibility for one of his books in passing… a possibility that ended up not materializing, because that's how the industry works… and the next time they spoke, he acted vaguely like a man betrayed. That sort of reflexive rationalization made life livable for some people, gave them illusions of a better life to work toward, but Shirley found such self-serving delusions just plain sad.

*   *   *

CHAPTER NINE:

LOOSE BALLS

Corporal Rick Shaw removed his helmet and ran his heavily calloused fingers over his government-issue haircut. He and his small military group of less than twelve soldiers had sustained some heavy fire in the section of Korea where they were stationed. They were advancing on/retreating from the Chinese/North Koreans, when suddenly, the firing stopped. For the first few seconds, the silence unnerved him more than the steady percussion of the shelling, but seconds turned into minutes, and the temptation to relax lingered. Rick tried not to get too comfortable, but the old cliché about war really was true: long stretches of boredom separated by moments of sheer terror. At least they found cover at the tree line before anybody got hit.

He'd stepped in a particularly muddy section of the rice paddy (cabbage patch?) they'd been crossing when they started to take fire, and ended up sinking up to his knee. If this really turned into a significant stretch of calm, he badly needed to dry his feet. He also needed to check for nicks and cuts on his legs, because he suspected that someone had recently fertilized this part of the field, and one part shit mixed with two parts open-wound was a recipe for an infection. That bodily inventory would have to wait, though, until he was 100% certain that they had reached a lull. For now, he would occupy his time checking his equipment.

"Hey, Shaw," Private Hatcher said, planting the but of his rifle in the ground and easing down onto the wet log that Rick already occupied. Hatcher had joined the company six days ago from the base where they were stationed. He still had the 24-hour-a-day, deer in headlights look about him, but he seemed like the competent and careful sort: two qualities that counted for a hell of a lot more than a winning personality when taking fire in a shit field. "Care if I join you?"

Rick shrugged; there didn't seem any other options since Hatcher had already sat down. "Suit yourself," he said. "Ain't my log."

Hatcher struck Rick as the last sort of person who should get stuck out in this mess. He had a brain, and looked so goddamn young, with the kind of soft face that wouldn't show a five o'clock shadow until six… the next day. This whole experience was going to leave its share of scars on the poor kid. "How're you holding up?" Hatcher asked.

Rick shrugged again. He wasn't the self-reflective type, so he didn't consider that question much without prompting; he held up well enough to survive, no more and no less. Once he got home, he could drown any of the remaining anxiety in a fifth of Kentucky bourbon. Now that he thought about it, though, he could have used a cigarette. "I've seen worse," he said, trying to sound authoritative. "Least nobody got hit. Was this your first time in the heavy shit?"

"Yeah," Hatcher admitted, letting out a mirthless laugh. "Nothing they put you through in Basic prepares you for the real thing."

"Ain't that the truth," Rick said, sliding the rucksack off his shoulder so he could reach inside and retrieve his last pack of Lucky Strikes he bought at the PX, what seemed like a month ago. "It's toasted!" the cellophane pack proclaimed. Aren't we all? Rick thought. He shook two loose with practiced efficiency and offered one to Hatcher. "You got nothin' to be ashamed of," he said with the squat, filterless cigarette pressed between his lips. "You did real good out there. You can always catch some bad *luck, no matter how careful you are, but the key is to pick up something each time, something different and little. A half a second here or a few inches there is the difference between surviving this shit and getting your head blown off."*

"Thanks, Shaw," Hatcher said with a slightly awkward smile. He leaned forward and let Rick light the cigarette with the silver Zippo that Rick normally kept strapped to his helmet. "What's your first name, anyway?"

"Corporal," Rick said, evenly, and released a jet of blackish smoke from the corner of his mouth. When it came to unfiltered cigarettes, you really couldn't beat Lucky Strikes.

"No, seriously," Hatcher persisted, with heart-wrenching earnestness. Rick would have liked to find the guy who sent this kid out here and ram a grenade up his ass. "I feel weird calling you by your last name or your rank."

Rick shook his head. "Don't get close to people out here, there's no percentage in it," he warned and waited for Hatcher to nod, which he did, a little sadly. The look made Rick feel like he kicked the poor kid's puppy. "Okay, fuck it. It's 'Rick,' not that it matters."

The look of recognition lit up Hatcher's face in mid-inhale. "Wow. Rick Shaw comes to Korea."

"Tell me about it," Rick said, smirking. He'd taken a lot of flak for it, but not so much in the field. Out here, your name could be Blimpo McFuckimself and no one cared as long as you could keep your shit together when the shooting started. "If this were Germany, at least it might take people a couple minutes to catch on."

"If this were Germany…" Hatcher began but didn't allow himself to finish. "Why don't you go by 'Richard'?"

"Because that's one step away from 'Dick Shaw,' which sounds like some kind of oriental condom," Rick explained, then added, "and it makes it look like I'm embarrassed."

"Fair enough," Hatcher countered. The delicious, rolled Carolina tobacco didn't seem to make him any less tense, though. Maybe he wasn't a regular smoker.

"I appreciate you telling me… because I have to admit something to you…" Jesus Christ, *Rick muttered internally, but even he wasn't prepared when Hatcher finished his thought, "… I'm really a woman." That was half a second before the sniper's bullet disintegrated her face.*

*   *   *

Derrick woke up the next morning, read his email, and tried to distract himself from the idea of one of his books getting made into a movie. He drank a large cup of coffee and typed three pages on the laptop before his momentum ran out and he decided to walk to the gym. Jogging down the stairs to the hotel lobby, his head swam pleasantly from the productivity-high. He almost made it past the front door of El Cantina, the Mexican restaurant located about a block away from the hotel, before he thought of a phrase he should have changed. He made it two blocks before he decided to junk the whole stupid idea. What did he know about the Korean War? He'd been in the country a little over twenty-four hours. Whatever he came up with, some Korean War vet would probably read it and get offended. Hopefully, he could sweat the stupid out of his system at the gym, get back to work after lunch, and create something that provided a lasting contribution to society.

Derrick walked down the sidewalk staring at a map drawn in blue ink on the back of a square napkin. The morning was only a little chilly, but the humidity made for a soupy atmosphere. The temperature must have hovered in the mid-forties (whatever the equivalent was in Celsius), but the steely clouds stretched to the horizon in all directions and just seemed to radiate damp. A modest gym actually sat in the basement of the hotel, but one day's use cost almost as much as the room. Yesterday, a Korean kid working the register at the Itaewon Dunkin' Doughnuts informed Derrick that there was a gym that charged the equivalent of $5 per day and sat about six blocks away from the hotel. As was the case with most international cities, Seoul liked to soak its foreign tourists, so if you got away from the "international" section of town, prices improved dramatically. It took about five minutes of broken English and ink pen diagrams for Derrick to come by this information.

With the race only a few days away, it wasn't like Derrick needed to workout in order to build endurance: he was in as good a shape as he could be for this race, for good or ill, and doing a lot of cardio would just wear him out. He did, however, need to keep his muscles and joints functional. He anticipated lifting a few light weights and riding the exercise bike for half an hour so that his body didn't completely go to slag. That was the plan… but as it turned out, this jaunt to the gym presented him with the best distraction he could hope for, because a visit to a Korean locker room provided his Westernized mind with an experience far more bizarre than a trip to the DMZ.

In the lobby of the building that housed the gym, there sat a front desk. He paid his 5,000 won (about $5 at the current exchange rate) and received what looked like a receipt from the smiling, artificially red-haired girl working the counter. The words on the receipt were written in Korean (of course), but through some monosyllabic exchanges and elaborate gesticulations, she informed him that he needed to take that scrap of paper to the fourth floor. As he turned to leave, he remembered to utter the Korean word for "thank you." She smiled broadly and performed a short bow, which made Derrick feel smarter than he had since he got three stars and a smiley face on his third grade spelling test.

On the fourth floor, the tile hallway ended a few yards from the staircase, and then a slightly raised wooden floor started. Over in the corner, in a small section of tile about the size of a broom closet, an older, mostly bald gentleman sat on a stool, shining shoes, so Derrick guessed that this was the floor's sacred threshold, beyond which, no footwear could tread. Even though he totally never got the Asian stockinged feet fetish (Do they somehow manage to step in a lot of dog shit around here?), he obediently removed his street shoes (which were just former regular running shoes that looked fine but had little tread or cushioning remaining). He picked up his shoes and walked past a couple rows of shoe lockers where one was expected to place one's street shoes, but he only brought one pair of athletic shoes with him that morning, and his cultural sensitivity only extended so far.

After the shoe locker chamber ended, the real locker room began. He carefully watched the Korean guy standing in front of him as the man waited to access the locker room. The customer wore a shiny, silver suit and a haircut that couldn't have required more than a salad bowl and thirty seconds to complete, and he handed a fifty-something guy behind a desk a slip of paper and received a key. Derrick did the same and got a key to Locker 21. There were about ten aisles of lockers in the room, and his sat located on the far left corner. The front desk apparently sold assorted other wares, ranging from juice boxes and disposable razors to shampoo and sleeveless undershirts: in other words, everything necessary for a good workout. Although Derrick found the sale of toothbrushes especially amusing, the reaction had little time to flourish, because the moment he stepped into the locker room proper, the visual avalanche of nude Korean men that met his gaze downright unnerved him.

There were at least a dozen of them in there (and even more lurking in the aisles), from teenagers to white-haired men, from firm to paunchy, but they all had two things in common: they were all undeniably Korean, and they were all naked as jaybirds. Several of them carried hand towels, but no one used said towels to cover up their swaying genitals. Stranger still, none of the visible men seemed to be *doing* anything. A few were cleaning up, blow-drying their hair and whatnot, a few were strolling to the gigantic sauna that sat on the other side of a pair of glass doors, and a few were just hanging out and talking. Most of these things could be accomplished with pants on, even amid the thick, oppressive heat of the sauna-adjacent locker room. Derrick attributed his reaction to cultural differences, just something he was unaccustomed to… and to be honest, nudity, per se, never really bothered him. It was just that he'd never considered nudity a goal unto itself. Here, though, nudity seemed to provide an actual ends, not a means, as in, "Honey, I'm going down to the gym to hang out naked for a while." And, yes, cultural sensitivity be damned, it struck him as a little goofy.

On the far side of the locker room, over by the water cooler, three black, fake leather sofas sat positioned in a "C" formation around a flat-screen TV. The program on the TV featured several Korean males jamming their mouths with stuff wrapped in leaves, seemingly in ecstasy. Four Korean men intently watched the program, all of them naked with their bare asses planted on the sofa vinyl. As he strolled past on his way to the locker, Derrick's first thought was, "Good thing they didn't choose white couches." His second thought was, "Good thing I took my shoes off, I wouldn't want to contaminate this downright surgical atmosphere.

A few glances passed over Derrick as he strode toward his assigned locker, but no accusatory stares landed. Being the anomaly… the interloper… didn't bother Derrick; he always felt out of place. It would have felt more awkward had they been warm and accepting, because he'd never shaken the hand of a naked man. He sighed and shuffled over to the aisle where Locker 21 sat. His brain probably hummed along at about 75% of its normal operating capacity, better than the day before, but besides the unreality of the situation, the characteristic jet-lagged sluggishness still lingered, such that his sleeping schedule consisted of two four-hour naps over the course of the day. He wasn't terribly worried, though. As long as he recovered by race day, everything would be fine; he had no place to be and nothing special to do beforehand.

Surprisingly, the only occupant of the aisle of lockers was a fat, hairy white dude, nude except for his dark brown socks. However, unlike the rest of the denizens of the locker room, this guy was in the process of getting dressed. Since Derrick hadn't seen a truly obese person in a couple days, he found it a little jarring. "Hey," the guy said after making a split-second of eye contact with Derrick. The single-syllable word took forever to emerge, and his accent was distinctly non-American.

"Hi," Derrick replied, stepping past the man to his locker. It seemed a little weird talking to a stranger in this situation, like an informal meeting of the White Guy Club, but he supposed that, in a foreign land, you found your conversation where you could. Thankfully, their lockers stood a few spaces apart; Derrick hated being wedged next to the only other person in the locker room and both parties having to reach around one another in various states of undress.

"Where ya from?" the guy asked, casually. Derrick wasn't much for placing accents, but this guy sounded neither British nor Australian. Appropriately, Derrick also wasn't much for adopting accents. He lived in Brooklyn for almost three years and never once pronounced the hot, caffeinated drink "kwaw-fee."

"United States," Derrick replied. He always considered it a little self-indulgent to refer to it as "America," what with there being two continents using that name. After a full second of silence, he considered that should ask where the guy was from, even though he really didn't care. "And you?"

"Wales," the guy said, pulling on a pair of white briefs with an exhausted elastic band. "You an English teacha?"

"No, I'm just a tourist," Derrick explained as he hung his backpack on a hook in the locker and removed a pair of workout shorts and a T-shirt he got for completing a race in Montreal. After a second of contemplating the appropriate thing to say, he asked, "Are you an English teacher?"

"Yeah, over at the University," the guy said, nodding in the general direction of what Derrick presumed was a university. They went on like this for a couple minutes, two strangers chatting for no other reason than that they might not get to again for the near future. Nothing useful came out of it, just the pleasant sensation of being recognized as existing.

Derrick got dressed, slid his shoes on in the stairwell at the back of the locker room, and climbed a flight of stairs to reach the weight room. Only a few things about the fifth floor struck him as especially strange. First, the gym seemed to have a uniform: grey T-shirts with blue sleeves for men and grey T-shirts with pink sleeves for women. So, it was kind of like a maternity ward that way. He didn't have a chance to notice this earlier, what with everyone being nude down in the locker room. Second, the gym members struck him as a little older than he expected. There were hardly any people younger than him; maybe retirees were the only ones who had the time or spare income to obtain gym memberships.

A pair of quite lovely young Korean girls walked briskly on the treadmills over in the cardio section of the room. Petite. Long, black flowing hair. Skin that could only be described as "alabaster," untainted by the bodily desecration known as "tattooing" that American women seemed to think punctuated their individuality, despite the fact that ink-gun art only looked good on Russian gangsters. He couldn't help but stare from time to time as he used the leg extension, leg press, and leg curl machines, and they still strutted along to their hearts' content when he adjourned over to the elliptical trainer. Usually, he gazed at them through the safety of one of the many mirrors inscribing the room, but he couldn't decide whether this made him a pervert. He had no idea how old they were, because he could guess the ages of trees more accurately than the ages of Asian women. These two could be anywhere from fifteen to twenty-five. Basking in their peripheral loveliness for over an hour made the transition all the more jarring when he finished his workout and returned to the locker room and its sea of exposed genitals.

Derrick decided to put off showering until he returned to his hotel room. In part, this was because his high level of cardiovascular conditioning meant that he could avoid profuse sweating in all but the most intense workouts. In part, though, he wasn't exactly sure how the process worked; it wouldn't have surprised him to learn that all the locker room's occupants had to pile into a collective Jacuzzi and use the same water and loofa. Either way, he would only have to wait ten minutes to shower back at the room, less if he jogged the distance. As he pulled his loose-fitting jeans over his workout shorts, a second occupant strolled into the aisle. Another foreigner.

A conversation much like the last one ensued, with Derrick taking on the role of greeter last played by the obese Welsh guy. The new guy was in his late twenties or early thirties and from Cameroon (which Derrick, admittedly, could not have found on a map of Africa). He was thin, looked about 5'8", and sported a shaved head. "What is this? The 'Foreigner Aisle'?" Derrick quipped after the shallow introductions. "The only other foreigner I've seen here had a locker in this aisle, too."

"I don't know that it's the foreigner aisle," the new guy said in his sing-songy accent as he unbuttoned his gray, long-sleeved shirt, "so much as the non-Asian aisle." Judging from the guys arms, he was built thin with a lot of lean muscle; the Welsh guy could have swallowed him whole.

Making the reflexive evaluation that runners unconsciously make, Derrick decided that, given a minimum of training, the Cameroonian (Cameroonese? Camerquois?) would probably destroy him in a race. When Derrick's eyes traveled back to the guy's face, he saw that the guy was smiling in a way that meant that he thought his previous statement was funny, but not that he was joking; it was a knowing smile.

"Why would they keep the foreigners… non-Asians separate?" Derrick asked as he snapped the clasp closed on his backpack. He assumed it was "soft apartheid" (his understanding was that Asian cultures tended to be unabashedly xenophobic) but he didn't want to assume something like that out loud.

The guy's abundant brow wrinkled. "Seriously? You see how they like to go free style in here!" He waited for the flicker of understanding to ignite in Derrick's eyes. When it arrived, the new guy let loose a cackle eerily reminiscent of the black actor wearing the white suit in those old "Don't you feel good about 7 Up?" commercials from when Derrick was a kid. He added, a little too loud, "Sometimes it's like I'm Clint Eastwood in the *Dirty Harry* movie!"

*   *   *

CHAPTER TEN:

INFLATING THE BUBBLE

Captain Rick Shaw gripped the top of Genevieve's swelling bodice as he pressed against her from behind. She could feel his heavily calloused hands squeezing the soft flesh of her bosom. "I be giving all of Red Beard's treasure for these, M'Lady," he snarled into her ear. She turned to slap him, but then her gaze met that of his lone remaining eye, whose deep blue color brought back the memory of the ocean outside of her beloved Nantucket home on a calm day. After a moment that seemed to last forever, she inhaled every bit of his swarthy scent. The image of her late husband faded, and she collapsed into the embrace of Rick Shaw's powerful arms.

*　　　　　*　　　　　*

"I can't write romance," Derrick admitted into the headset's mouthpiece. His elaborate plan of distracting himself away from hope's glossy temptations didn't last long once he returned from the gym; by the time he'd finished showering, he'd begun contemplating how long it would take him to save enough money to buy a cottage in southern France. He'd never been to southern France, but how bad could it be? He could buy one in a nice, peaceful place, and he could go there and write and try to learn French. Maybe it would have a vineyard, but he knew less about wine than he did about French, so that would be a tentative detail at best, but surely his neighbors would know about wine, right?

The intrusive thoughts wouldn't have overwhelmed him were there still a job to occupy his mind, but without that regular eight hours of mindlessness to descend into, they stacked onto one another like Lego blocks. He decided to contact Shirley via the Skype program on his computer once he finished toweling off. Despite his complete lack of social skills, Derrick thought that hearing her voice might give him a better idea of where things really stood with the book/movie situations. After settling into that plan, though, he quickly realized that he would have to wait until 11 p.m. Korean Standard Time before calling in order to ensure that Shirley had arrived in her New York office. So wait he did, staring at the clock, trying to will away the minutes like a heroin addict going through withdrawal.

"That's what you said last time, when you tried to submit something for that stupid novel contest," she reminded him, absently. There was a couple-second delay on the call's audio that made the conversation naturally choppy and demanded more effort than normal. Derrick told himself that that was her problem. "What made you think this time would be different?

Derrick ignored the question. In truth, he'd been thinking a lot more about Sylvia than he had in years. Maybe that got him feeling amorous. "I think my problem comes from never having a read any romance," he said, shifting around in his unpadded, wooden hotel desk chair.

"Or had any," she quipped.

"Funny," he replied, neglecting to remind Shirley of her spinster status. It would have felt good to fire that shot across the bow, but both ends of the conversation would have deteriorated beyond repair. Instead, he took on the role of the adult and just absorbed the insult. "I've really missed your rapier wit."

"I'm sorry," she said, automatically, without sounding remotely sorry. "Cleverly named protagonists just don't work well for romance, unless it's an obvious euphemism. I supposed you just have to use a lot of clichés."

"I don't think finding the right phrasing is the issue," he told her. He couldn't remember whether she had dabbled in romance during her attempt at writing. Somehow he found it nearly as implausible to contemplate as his attempt. Shirley was too – what's the word? *Mercenary?* – to write romance. In any case, he rarely asked her for writing advice, because he never knew when it would stop. Now, he was stuck, though, like he'd never been stuck before. "I just can't get into it. Same thing when I tried to turn it into a war story. I need more than a name and a basic genre. It needs a hook, a soul." As he allowed the silence to float between them, an idea popped into his head. "Maybe I can do something with that: a romance novel by a guy who can't write romance."

"That might be funny," she offered, somewhat convincingly, "but I would strongly advise against writing too much of yourself into the book. Author's think books about authors are great, but that's because they're authors. Would you name the author 'Rick Shaw'?"

"Yeah, I still think that's funny," Derrick assured her.

"Well, not to beat a dead horse, but you have to have a *reason* to include that name," Shirley told him. "It has to fit into the grand scheme. I mean, I think the term 'Torture Porn' is hysterical, but I'm not going to base my next book around that name unless I have a very good reason."

"Are you still writing?" Derrick asked, audibly surprised.

"Yeah, of course I'm still writing," she said, defensively. It was the first genuine response he'd gotten out of her. She added, "I'm a writer."

Derrick shrugged. He seriously doubted she'd strung together more than a paragraph of fiction in the years that he'd known her, but like he gave a shit; she could call herself a writer, a cowboy, or the fucking queen of England if she wanted. The skill set of an agent was not the skill set of a writer, and in relation to his life, her percentage was based on the former. "Yeah, I know you wrote, but you usually refer to it in the past-tense, so I wasn't sure—"

"Nooo, I still do it."

"How does that work," he asked, leaning back precariously far in the stiff hotel chair. The wire of his headset became taught, so he stopped leaning. "I mean, does somebody else in the agency represent you?"

"We can represent ourselves, but we have to do it on our own time, and we have to use pen names." It was a rehearsed response, delivered with a speed that belied her discomfort with the topic. Maybe he'd asked about it before; asking questions and forgetting the answers was one of his more annoying habits. The proximity of her aspiration to her occupation had to frustrate her more than a little, to still cling to that dream but surround yourself with people who have achieved your dream to varying degrees. He didn't remember them talking much about her heart's desire. They probably did, probably at the beginning, during the get-to-know-you phase, but he didn't remember the details. "Look, I thought you'd be a little more interested in all the things I've done for you lately."

"Eh," Derrick said, rubbing his forehead, "I have a tendency to… get ahead of myself on these things, so I'm staying cautiously optimistic, y'know? I'll start counting it as happening when I see something signed."

"Well, that's a shitty attitude to take," Shirley shot back, sounding almost insulted. "News like this doesn't come along very often. I should know." She gave the comment a second to sink in. Was she referring to her capacity as an agent or her capacity as a writer? Maybe both. "Think about it this way: this is one step toward permanent financial stability and literary immortality. Your life would irrevocably change for the better."

Even as she spoke, images of this better, more beautiful, happier life started to gather in Derrick's head like storm clouds, but he blinked them away. *Storm clouds,* he thought. *Appropriate metaphor: objectively beneficial but subjectively ominous.* "I try not to think about it," he said, evenly. "I guess I don't want to get disappointed."

"At least go out and have a beer tonight… on me," she said, her tone changing to positively sympathetic. "And for god's sake, congratulate yourself on sticking with it and making it this far."

"I don't drink before a race," Derrick told her. "The carbonation can give you cramps."

Shirley sighed, causing a rasp in the mouthpiece of her office phone. "You lead a very joyless existence, you know that?"

"I prefer the word, 'Spartan,'" he said, a slight smile crawling across his lips, "but, yeah, my lifestyle takes some getting used to."

"Are you having fun in Korea, at least?"

"I don't think Korea is supposed to be fun. It seems more 'character-building' than fun,'" he replied, glancing out his room's window at the dark grey sky. It was night, but the light from ten million people made the sky gunmetal grey. "Did you know that South Korea has the highest suicide rate in the industrial world?"

"Really?" she said, suddenly about 20% more animated. "Higher than North Korea?"

"I said, 'industrial world.' I don't think North Korea has many trains you can throw yourself in front of."

"Why is it so high? Do they say?"

Derrick leaned forward and rested his elbows on the desktop. He didn't, in fact, know what *they* said, but he'd actually given this issue a lot of thought. "Well, I haven't checked this with the Bureau of Tourism, but I think that, on one hand, honor suicide is practically a national sport, like in Japan. Plus, they put a lot of pressure on their kids at an early age. And there's a big emphasis on duty over personal fulfillment. That's kind of a bad combination. Plus, in my admittedly limited experience, it's constantly overcast here. Reminds me of Michigan."

"God," Shirley said. He could almost hear her shudder over the phone line. "I've never been to Michigan, but it sounds awful."

This drew a smirk out of Derrick. Like most New Yorkers, Shirley never traveled west of the Hudson River unless it was onboard a 747 bound for LAX. As a result, she viewed the middle of the country the way hobbits viewed Mordor. "Well, I hope our conversation won't cause you nightmares later tonight."

"Oh, the coffee and cigarettes keep me from sleeping deep enough to dream." She meant this as a joke, but Shirley's throat let out a wheeze that she probably didn't detect as she shifted into her business voice. "Seriously, though. Try to have a good time. You're living a life a lot of people never get to, and it's about to get better. Whatever financial limitations you have are about to disappear. You won't have to work those stupid part-time jobs to travel anywhere. You might be able to make some long-term investments… if that's something you're interested in. Just promise me that you'll relax a little bit, and promise me that you'll accept the fact that something good has happened."

"I promise that I'll think about doing that," Derrick offered, "but thanks for the pep talk, coach."

Shirley sighed. "If that's the only promise I can get." She struck him as awfully pushy for someone whose position at the literary agency he'd (presumably) just helped secure.

"That's the only promise you can get," he assured her.

"Well, you have a good day."

"It's a little after eleven p.m. here, but thanks. You, too."

*   *   *

The next morning, in the weight room, Derrick ran across the guy from Cameroon. He wore black sweatpants and a grey T-shirt featuring Japanese writing and a picture of a yellow, cartoon bird with a baseball cap. It took Derrick two sets on the shoulder press machine to remember that the guy's name was "Phillip." He was terrible with names. He knew the old memory trick of saying the person's name three times in conversation upon meeting them and never questioned its efficacy, but that tactic always made him feeling like he was selling boat insurance.

They both said hello. Derrick wondered whether Phillip ever went by "Phil," but he doubted it. In his limited experience with people from central Africa, they tended to follow the European tradition of incorporating the full name. Besides sounding classier, since their traditional names often stretched on for ten syllables, it must have seemed kind of lazy to shorten "Christopher" to "Chris."

"So," Derrick asked after Phillip finished his set of twelve reps on the adjacent pull-down machine, "What brings you to sunny Seoul?"

"Work," Phillip said. "I teach English at a school near here." He performed an elaborate head tilt that nearly mimicked the Welsh guy from the previous day. Maybe they worked at the same school.

"Jesus Christ," Derrick said. "Does anybody who isn't from here have an occupation other than English teacher?"

"American military," Phillip reminded him while focusing his gaze on the rising stack of weights. "Their presence is rather conspicuous. What they lack in numbers, they make up for in Saturday night volume."

"Ain't that the truth," Derrick agreed, even though he'd never spent a Saturday night in Seoul. A fifty-something, barefoot Korean man with slumped shoulders crossed in front of them on his way over to the dumbbell rack. Derrick continued to talk, but his eyes stayed fixed to the man's feet. "I'm staying down in Itaewon, and I've been waking up at five-something every morning because of the time change, and those loud bastards are still rolling down the street. I'm on the tenth floor and I can still hear them like they're right outside my window."

"It's worse at the restaurants," Phillip informed him. "I think that sometimes they forget where they are. Very ethnocentric."

The barefoot guy started jerking a ten kilogram dumbbell over his head in some awkward lift Derrick never saw before that almost looked like he was starting a particularly stubborn lawnmower. Besides wreaking havoc on his vertebrae, if that weight slipped out of his hand on the down-stroke, it would turn his foot into cream-of-bone. None of the three personal trainers milling about responded, though, so the act of lifting random shit in random ways must have been acceptable.

"I know what you mean," Derrick said, then nodded to indicate the barefoot lifter. "Take this guy, for instance. It's a contest to see whether he slips a disc or breaks his first foot, but I'll be damned if I'm going to stop him."

"How culturally sensitive of you!" Phillip said, grinning. He grinned a lot, and his large, white teeth made his smile especially noticeable... almost iridescent. *It must be his default expression*, Derrick thought. Derrick's own default expression was probably best described as "pensive." "But you would not intervene on someone who could understand you, yes?"

Derrick tried to digest the awkwardly worded question for a couple seconds, then blindly offered, "Probably not?" Answering the question accurately concerned him more than its implications; he was the live-and-let-live sort, even when it became detrimental. He strongly believed in the idea that people have the right to destroy themselves, because there are worse fates than death floating out there in the world. In any case, his answer must have satisfied Phillip because their conversation briefly shifted toward a discussion of local coffee. After another minute or so, they parted ways when Derrick went to do some dips and Phillip walked over to the comically limited dumbbell rack. Within ten minutes, though, they were seated at adjacent, upright exercise bikes.

"So, what do you do for a living?" Phillip asked, pedaling significantly faster than Derrick. "I assume that you neither soldier professionally nor teach English-as-a-second-language, yes?"

Derrick inhaled deeply. Were he a savvier businessman, he would have launched into his book spiel every time someone new offered up that question. People, for whatever reason, like to associated themselves with someone famous, even if that person is only sort of famous, even if they'd never heard of the sort-of-famous-person, and buying the novel of the guy they pedaled next to in the gym allowed them to do this… even if they never read it. Derrick, however, was not a savvy businessman, and whether due to a sense of misplaced etiquette or massive self-loathing, he found blatant self-promotion incredibly boorish. "I work in a factory," he said to Phillip, but didn't like that answer, either. It sounded a little too much like he considered himself blue collar (which he didn't deserve), so he added, "But mainly I'm living off of the residuals of a book I wrote ten years ago."

"No kidding?" Phillip said, illuminating even further. "What book?"

"It was just some book I wrote in college. *Dead Man in Sheets.* It's about a guy who thinks he's the reincarnation of Jesus. Wackiness ensues."

"I have never heard of it," Phillip admitted, "but it sounds interesting. Especially the part about wackiness ensuing."

"It's okay," Derrick said, somewhat reluctantly. "I mean, when you consider that I wrote it when I was a kid."

"You really know how to entice someone into buying your book," Phillip said, grinning again as he swayed a few inches back and forth to the rhythm of his pedaling. He probably could have maintained that pace for hours.

Derrick leaned forward and increased the resistance on the bike. "Yeah, well, that's what agents are for."

*   *   *

CHAPTER ELEVEN:

STASIS

Shirley pushed closed her apartment's front door. She turned the deadbolt lock, slid her feet out of her comfortable leather loafers, dropped her cloth work bag loaded with two manuscripts into a chair by the door and stalked into the kitchen. Her feet thumped against the hardwood floor in a distinctly unladylike manner. Back when she lived in Hoboken, she had thick, wall-to-wall carpet, and it was wonderful. After a hard day's work, she could knead those fibers with her toes and massage the stress away. Technically, she could install carpeting in her current domicile, but what kind of idiot installs carpet over perfectly good hardwood floors? Especially in the city?

Shirley stopped by the refrigerator on her way to the cupboard and poured herself half a glass of red wine into one of her white wine glasses. Who cares if the wine didn't get a chance to breathe? Now was time for alcohol, not taste. Pippa, her calico cat, rubbed up against her beige pant leg, jealous of the attention her wine glass was receiving, at least until she got fed. She must've been there since Shirley walked in the door, but Shirley just noticed her.

Unlike many of her self-consciously sophisticated friends, Shirley owned a TV, a nice flat-screen number that she bought back when flat-screens were relatively cutting-edge... during that twelve-month window before the high-definition avalanche. Still, she didn't turn it on very much. Most of her viewing of TV programs took place through the internet at work. The playlist consisted mostly of news programs, and really, so long as it wasn't pornography, no one at the agency cared. She needed relative silence when reading through manuscripts, but the audio drone served as a mildly engaging background stimulus while she sat at her desk and filled out forms or sent out letters.

On this night, with her cat fed, she sat in the dim light of her Rooms-To-Go living room set and listened to the twin sounds of her cat eating in the kitchenette and the mercifully non-honking traffic from outside. *I hate my life*, she thought as she stared at the dark version of herself in the broad, flat, dormant TV screen. If she looked close enough, that version would appear just as it did the last time she stared at it, except a little older. She took another snort of wine, and having settled in for the night, the sensation reminded her that she needed to buy new red wine glasses, since the last one broke a month ago (she could taste the difference when she drank wine from the wrong type of glass... she swore it). How many people consciously hated their lives at least once per week? Given the stagnation of real wages over the last thirty years, coupled with an ever-increasing credence given to the idea that anything is possible if we just work hard enough, she would guess the number to be high... maybe 25 percent and growing. She was something around an every-other-day person, herself.

She once picked up a copy of one of those self-help psychology books at work (there were always spare copies of freshly printed books lying around) and took it with her on a flight to Portland. Although she typically found that genre of writing useless to the point of insult, that particular book made one stellar point that stuck with her ever since: our dissatisfaction with our life is typically the result of a large disparity between where we are (our *situation*) and where we feel like we should be (our *aspiration*). She never thought she would be alone, pushing fifty, and preparing a résumé just in case she got shit-canned in the next week from a job to which she'd devoted her existence for fifteen years. Granted, no one in the history of the world likely ever planned for that particular eventuality, but for her, it marked a complete collapse of her personal and professional life.

Shirley always wanted to be important. Most people do, but she was explicit about it. From the time she was sixteen and saw Zbigniew Brzezinski give an interview on PBS, she wanted to be someone who, when she spoke, people listened to what she had to say. She liked writing and got A's in English class, so that would be her vehicle. From that moment on, she worked hard and worked smart and made all the right connections, but always remained a couple talent points (or let's face it, beauty points) away from pulling off a writing career. At some point, everybody who isn't born into the industry has to take some chances if they're ever going to make it. When you decide that it's your time to make The Leap, you either catch hold of the proverbial brass ring or you don't. What most people don't realize is that, when you miss that brass ring, you fall... and the drop is precipitous. You don't get that time and money and self-esteem back. You don't land safely and pretend that that's what you wanted all along. Shirley didn't quite splatter on the pavement, but instead of being a literary star, circumstance left her with a

lone option that kept her in the game: become a literary scavenger. It
would let her cultivate more connections and allow her to make the next
leap from a safer distance. Sure, it would… at least that's what she told
herself at the time.

Amadeus had always been one of her favorite movies, but she had
problems watching it these last few years, ever since Derrick blindly
stumbled into her life. Whenever she came across it now, she always felt
like Salieri: petty and envious of the truly talented. But, Jesus, if Derrick's
life's story was Amadeus (which it wasn't, but y'know… for the sake of
comparison), she wouldn't even be Salieri, because at least he was a real
artist; she'd be Mozart's shrill mother-in-law, always voicing her
dissatisfaction with him, while at the same time, trying to sponge off him
for all it was worth.

She wanted big things out of life, and that's why she hated
Derrick so damned much. It wasn't personal… granted, hate is always
personal, but her hate for him metastasized mostly because of what he
stood for. He wasn't a "bad guy," just some schlub who backed into a
writing career, and who didn't have the drive or the basic wherewithal to
sustain it. If Shirley had written Dead Man in Sheets, you can bet your ass
she'd have been pimping that fucking book to anyone she stood next to
on the subway. She would have bought a bus, converted it into a
billboard on wheels advertising that book, and drove it around midtown
Manhattan during every morning and afternoon rush hour. Derrick, on
the other hand, can barely manage to make it through a single interview
without slamming his own goddamn book for being flawed or incoherent
or… what was the immortal phrase he used in the NPR interview? "Just
me spouting my monkey-love."

Were she more self-reflective, Shirley might have wondered if,
deep down, she'd always wanted Derrick's career fail, even if it ended up

materially costing her, because if he couldn't follow up the success of
Dead Man, that would affirm that his existence as a writer was a fluke and
that the universe was cosmically unfair. Of course, if she wanted him to
fail, she was in a perfect position to make that desire a reality (consciously
or unconsciously). Had she realized these things, she might have
considered that she *needed* to hate Derrick; she would have to believe in
God to hate Him, and it depressed her too damn much to hate herself.
Derrick could serve as her scapegoat, in the Biblical sense, and suffer for
all her literary sins. Were she more self-reflective, she might have thought
about all these things, but accessing that depth of insight would require
above a tenth grade reading level, and most self-help psychology books
don't strive for that rarified air. Besides, a glass of wine made her more
bitter than reflective, and bitterness just made her regret all the mistakes
she made. *Two* glasses of wine on the other hand...

     *   *   *

Chapter Twelve:
Glial Cells

"My name… is Mister Shaw," Rick said as he wrote his name on the chalkboard in his chicken-scratch scrawl. He could have used the overhead projector or the dry-erase board located on the adjacent wall, but the staccato scraping sound made him feel like a teacher in the 1950's, a period of time when teachers were respected in his country. A low murmur rippled throughout the classroom, but even if the voices had been audible, he wouldn't have understood what they were saying. "This is English 100. And the first thing you need to know," he said, turning around and fully staring down the sea of unfamiliar faces, "is that there are no victims in this classroom."

The murmuring stopped, leaving the Korean words for "dirty American" hanging in the air. Rick turned to observe the temporarily silent, ragtag group of students that Fate had sent him. The Ministry of Education had dispatched Rick to the toughest school in all of Busan because they knew he was one of the best damn English instructors in the country. On an intellectual level, he had an idea of what to expect before he arrived, but reading the numeric data on a sheet of paper and attaching the meaning of that data to a wall of glowering humanity invoked two vastly different realities. Three of the male students sat in the back of the classroom with black T-

shirts and sunglasses, flashing the hand signals that indicated that they were junior representatives of the (Korean crime syndicate). Half the girls in the class looked as though they had third-trimester tummies wedged under the wooden desktops, and half the males appeared to be carrying knives, even though only one of them was actually sharpening his in plain sight. The knife-sharpener may have been trying to intimidate Rick, but it would take more than a teenager with a pig-sticker to overcome four years of Special Forces training.

Rick remembered his rules of public speaking, and since he couldn't find a friendly face upon which to focus, he picked out a spot on the back wall. "I don't care what prefecture you're from or whether your name is Park or Kim," he began, his voice strengthening with each word, "everyone has an equal opportunity in this class to learn English… and at the end of the semester, you're perfectly welcome to tell me to go fuck myself, as long as you use the correct verb tense."

*   *   *

"No, Korean high school girls don't get pregnant!" Phillip said, laughing. His tone was jolly, not demeaning, so Derrick didn't feel especially offended.

"They have sex, don't they?" Derrick said. The alternative seemed remote. They were teenagers, after all.

"Only if they have the money to go to a love hotel," Phillip insisted, still smiling. "The scenario is so implausible. High schools that teach English as a mandatory course would have students going to cram schools in the evening, not having sex, and having a pregnant teenager attending class would be a severe dishonor to the family." He paused for a breath. "Put it this way: I've been teaching here five years, and I've never once seen a visibly pregnant student, and that's at the university level."

"Hm. Sorry for my gross inaccuracies," Derrick said to Phillip and Phillip's Korean girlfriend with the unpronounceable name. The three of them had gone out to eat together, and they were all seated on the hardwood floor of one of the look-alike restaurants that littered the surrounding thirty square-miles. Derrick sat with his arms locked and his palms pressing against the section of floor immediately behind him, but his ass and back had already started to ache. Marathon training doesn't exactly give you a lot of natural cushion to work with when seated on hard objects, and with the surface of the table suspended a little over a foot off the ground, he couldn't exactly lean forward and rest his elbows next to his plate. "It was only a first draft."

Phillip waved it off. "That's nothing compared to the 'crime syndicate' reference," he assured Derrick.

The girlfriend picked up a plastic bottle of beer (brand name: "Hite") and started to pour some into Derrick's double-shot-sized "beer glass." He held up his hand and shook his head.

"You not drink alcohol?" the girlfriend said, sweetly. Everything she said had the most adorable tone. Derrick had heard that Korean women could be real bitchy behind closed doors, but in his limited experience, they all acted like the front desk worker at his hotel: so polite you wanted to tip them. This one was especially good at smiling or laughing whenever Phillip did the same.

"No," he explained. "I do, normally. I'm just running in the marathon on Sunday."

Her eyes lit up in recognition of something he said (probably the word "marathon"), but it was Phillip who replied. "Ah, yes, group masochism at its finest. Tell me, how fast do you expect to run?"

"I'm shooting for a 3:30, but I realistically expect to run about ten or fifteen minutes slower than that." Phillips eyebrows raised, and Derrick again wondered if Phillip could outrun him... right then. "It depends on... several factors." Fortunately, he stopped himself from describing the finer points of peristalsis while at the dinner table. It might only indicate the smallest possible improvement in his social skills, but as the saying goes, you have to crawl before you can walk.

"Why do you do that?" the girlfriend asked, using her arms to pantomime running. She continued smiling while she pumped her arms, which is something you just don't see often with high-level marathon running.

Derrick took a deep breath. This was why he could never date a non-native English speaker. More than anything, he wanted to give an accurate answer, but the answer to her question involved a complex narrative about parsing life up into memorable events and milestones that you could look forward to, and about self-loathing and the desire to, through force of will, forge yourself into a more disciplined, more worthy creature. He didn't want to spend five minutes explaining himself, though, or another five minutes going over it again to define the unfamiliar terms. So, he just smiled and said, "It's fun." The instant the words left his mouth, it felt like the lamest, most dishonest answer he could have spewed forth, and he knew the feeling would linger like the taste of bad coffee.

"Yes, people always look as though they're having a magnificent time during those," Phillip said, grinning.

"Well," Derrick reminded him, "you could make the same argument about sex." Once again, he stopped himself from making the social faux pas of mimicking an orgasm face.

"A valid point," Phillip replied, lifting his Dixie-Cup-sized beer glass in acknowledgement. He took a drink and turned to the girlfriend. "Derrick here is a professional writer." Then, without waiting for a reaction, turned back to Derrick, "Are you currently working on any projects?"

Derrick considered the question for a couple seconds before answering. "I suppose so," he said, finally. Phillip refutations of teen pregnancy and organized crime in Korea destroyed the possibility of having Rick Shaw work as a high school teacher in inner-city Busan, so the plot of the book once again descended into the mists of non-specificity. "It's more in the 'planning stages,' but it's something I'm spending time on, yeah."

"May I ask what it is?"

"I'm not totally sure," Derrick replied. He really didn't like talking about writing to non-writers. They didn't seem to understand that ideas didn't come out of a faucet; you couldn't force yourself to come up with a good idea. Strangely, people couldn't understand distance running, either, and, unlike writing, that was *all* about effort. "So far, I've only figured out the main character's name."

"Is that considered having the writer's block?"

"Not really," Derrick said, sliding a few inches out from under the table and shifting forward slightly so that he could transfer his weight and rest his elbows on his knees. Even this minimal movement made three of his vertebrae pop in relief. "It's just that, after my first book, I've been having difficulty coming up with anything even close to as good, and I think part of it is that I don't spend enough time planning; I just dive in and end up with something that wasn't worth my time."

"Were any of the other books published?"

"A couple, but they were kind of sympathy publications," Derrick admitted. "The publisher wasn't wild about them, but they thought they might be able to take advantage of the sales from the first one… kind of like, 'strike when the iron is hot' type of thing. It didn't work out real well, and I was starting to wonder if I hadn't destroyed my own reputation."

"That's a very depressing thought to have," Phillip admitted, and, on cue, his girlfriend took on an appropriately sorrowful countenance.

Derrick shrugged. "I'm a very depressing person." He knocked back another thimble-sized glass of water and set the glass down so that a female could refill it in the near future, as dictated by the cultural. He didn't know how anyone got drunk using that system; maybe the short glasses work for short people. The results spoke for themselves, though, because, boy howdy, did Koreans know how to drink. His first day in town, when he saw the group of middle-aged guys drinking bottles of rice wine at the crack of dawn, that turned out to be the norm, not the exception. Seoul alone must have a million high-functioning alcoholics, and based on the central role alcohol played in group behavior, it would have been social suicide to *not* drink like a fish. "Then, my agent calls and says that some movie studio is interested in making a movie from my first book... but I'm not sure what to think."

Phillip continued to look at him expectantly. When no additional information emerged, he said, "I think that sounds like fantastic news."

"It's early yet," Derrick assured him, staring at the pile of seaweed sitting on a white, rectangular plate in the middle of the table. When it first arrived, he didn't think he would like seaweed, but he tried a little, and it turns out that he was right: he didn't like seaweed. "These things usually fall through, and if that happens, I'm back at square one." He knew how that sounded out loud, of course, but he had to continually remind himself to keep his optimism guarded.

"Where is your end square?" Phillip asked.

Derrick blinked and returned to the present. "I'm sorry. What?"

Phillip's eyes searched the ceiling as he rephrased. "What are your career development goals?"

"I don't know," Derrick admitted. He looked down at his glass, hoping that Phillip's girlfriend would get the hint and refill it with some more water before he got dehydrated. "I try not to think too far in advance. I try to take things one day at a time, but I think to some extent, I worry about the future, or at least, I worry about the prospect of having to worry about the future."

"That sounds more like running from the future than living in the moment."

"Probably," Derrick said without really analyzing the veracity of the statement. "I doubt very many people would call what I'm doing 'living,' anyway." He winced. That comment broad-jumped over the line separating "guarded optimism" and "melancholy," which was an especially inappropriate shift to spring on two people he just met. Unless he wanted to start paying Phillip a therapist's salary, he needed to grab the controls and pull out of the nosedive. "Enough about me. How did you two meet?"

"She was a student in one of my classes," Phillip explained without hesitation. "Our attraction was immediate."
Derrick nodded and glanced over at the girlfriend, who demurred. "Can't you get in trouble for that?" he asked Phillip.

"Of course," Phillip said, "if anyone finds out, but no one got hurt and no one found out, and I don't regret our decision even slightly." The girlfriend gracefully rose to her feet in one fluid motion, still smiling shyly. She stopped to give a slight bow toward Derrick, then walked from the table with tiny steps.

After she crossed the room and disappeared through the door behind Derrick, he waited a couple seconds to ask, "Did I say something?"

"Of course not," Phillip assured him. "I believe she is using the lavatory." He took a sip of his beer. "It is a funny word, 'lavatory.' I prefer it to 'wash room,' like the Canadians say. Did you know that it came from the fact that Europeans had to use lavender to fight the toilet smell?"

"I did not," Derrick replied. Several seconds of silence passed and he reached across the table and poured himself some water. His lower back was killing him, unlike Phillip, who maintained his picket fence posture with no visible consequences. "She doesn't' talk much, does she?"

"Mercifully, no," Phillip said. "I don't intend that to sound negative. I quite like talking with her, and she's wonderfully patient in helping me with my Korean, but I've dated American women who cannot tolerate two seconds of silence." Derrick gave a knowing smile as he nodded in agreement. "Do you find it surprising that I have dated American women?"

"What? No," Derrick said, almost hurt by the accusation. How exactly did he convey that? Was it the nod? He knocked back the shot of water to buy himself some time. "No, I was just thinking about how an American woman would respond to hearing you say that." Phillip nodded, allowing Derrick to relax and stop worrying about sounding like a bigot. "No, I would think you're pretty successful with women. You have the whole self-assuredness thing down."

"That's an interesting way of putting it," Phillip said. "Specifically, because I thought you possessed that quality when we first met, but now I think quite the opposite."

"You think I'm not self-assured?" Derrick asked. He didn't know if the directness of the statement was a byproduct of a lack of language proficiency, or whether Phillip knew exactly what he was saying but had the luxury of playing it off as a lack of language proficiency. He would guess the latter. In any case, Derrick preferred bluntness; it didn't leave anything to read into. "I mean, I don't think I am, but I'm curious why I come off the way I do."

"You seem terrified of not being sure of yourself, so you make certain to always fake it," Phillip said as soon as Derrick finished his sentence. "It holds for a matter of minutes, but our true selves always come shining through, eventually." Phillips smiled. "Of course, I say this as if we've known one another for years."

"Can't argue with that, as much as I'd like to," Derrick replied, pouring himself another tiny glass of water since the last glass somehow failed to quench his thirst. He had made a conscious decision to fake confidence years go. It never got him many tangible positives, but it served a protective function: at least it kept people from viewing him as such a... victim. "I've never been sure of myself, and in my experience, the people who are so certain about everything are usually wrong. I know I don't have the answers to life, but I don't want to be one of those dead-certain jackasses driving off the cliff."

"What cliff?"

Derrick considered the question, and for some reason, remembered a comment that Shirley made years ago: that he wrote a lot of weak protagonists. His response was something along the lines of that it takes a certain amount of strength to admit that you don't know what you're doing. "Well, all I means is that overconfidence has a tendency to make every problem worse."

"I'll drink to that," Phillip said, raising his tiny glass of shitty, weak beer. It created a momentary feeling of understanding and fraternity, but then again, he probably would have drank to anything at that point.

*   *   *

The next morning, Derrick checked the red stick-numbers on the bedside digital clock and made a mental note that he was twenty-four hours away from the start of the marathon. The only thing he really had to worry about at this point, the only detail left to control, was what he decided to put in his body. In terms of diet, he had to eat things that he knew would pass out of his system in time for the race, and nothing that would upset the delicate harmony of his digestive tract. So, Mexican food was out… and so was Korean food. Good thing he was staying in Itaewon: he could eat fresh at Subway for both meals, even if a foot-long, oven-roasted chicken sub cost something like eleven bucks there.

With his head still thick and hazy from the valium he had popped two hours before bedtime, Derrick checked his email. Another message from Shirley. *I must be more popular than Mark Wahlberg in that office*, he thought. *All it took was a publication and a movie deal.* He felt a soft glow of happiness for Shirley, though. She'd worked as his agent for almost seven years, and in this economy, he was glad he could finally give her a little security at the agency. Perhaps anticipating a healthy dose of gratitude, he clicked on the message.

Derrick,

The agency is asking us to check with our clients about copyright transfers. Basically, it's like a will. A will supersedes it, of course, but most of our clients don't have the transfer of their book rights figured out in a legal fashion. On one hand, it's just a formality, but it's also not the kind of thing you want to regret later. I know you have some family issues, and I wouldn't want to assume anything. Just let me know who you want to get the rights to your books (published and unpublished) in the event of the unthinkable, our legal department can draw something up for you to sign, and we can play the fax game back and forth until it gets taken care of.

Still no word from the studio. I <u>tentatively</u> expect something early next week.
Good luck on your race.
Shirley

Derrick slouched into the flimsy, wooden, hotel desk chair. What an excellent, though untimely, question. Who did he want getting his books in "the event of the unthinkable"? Those books were bound to be his most lasting contribution to the world, however meager a contribution. As he mentioned to Phillip and (sort of) to Phillip's girlfriend, he tried to be the sort of person who focused on the present rather than the worries of the future or the regrets of the past. He was halfway there, most of the time... if only there weren't so damn many regrets. This seemed like a situation where it would be prudent to look forward. Even though it had yet to happen, Derrick had to assume that he could die, and he also had to assume that humanity would continue on, in some form or another, without him... at least for a while. So, who did he want to leave in charge of his modest legacy?

Shirley was right about his "family issues." Derrick's father died two weeks from Derrick's fifteenth birthday due to complications from a hip-replacement surgery. His mother married some rich guy with a yacht almost a year later (the guy had a bunch of other unnecessary shit, too, but that yacht represented everything else so perfectly; why the fuck do you need a yacht in Ohio?). He and his "parents" only saw one another once a year, for about three days ever Christmas. Mom and Burt both thought Derrick was a homosexual and a Communist, but Mom had the decency to not make the lifestyle accusations in the middle of dinner... at least public dinners.

Derrick probably would have severed ties with his mother and her yachting paramour long ago if his lone sibling hadn't left him with the responsibility of maintaining contact. He wished he could say that his older sister, Lisa, had cut ties as some sort of principled stand, but really, she just joined a cult... honest to Christ: an actual, factual fucking cult. He kept expecting to see her decomposing body stuffed into a solid-color track suit on the national news, but not all cults are suicide cults. She stopped talking to Mom and Burt when they stopped sending her money. Derrick had stopped taking their money after he graduated from high school and was preparing to ease out of the family, but then Lisa beat him to the fucking punch, leaving him holding the bag, mixaphorically speaking, as their mother's child. At least Lisa had the decency to not try to hit Derrick up for cash when raising money to build a new edition to the Benevolent Leader's summer home in Martha's Vineyard, but maybe that's because she couldn't find Derrick outside of cyberspace (they were Facebook friends... because cultists buy books, too). He didn't give a shit; he never liked Lisa, but strangely, it took him until he was about twenty to realize that he even had that option.

He could leave the books to a charity or a school, but if the sales dried up, that would look like some kind of sick joke. *Hey, orphans, I have a surprise for you: a big box of home-grown... nothing!* He could leave the rights to the English Department at his college... but given his checkered history there, and the fact that most of his contemporaries had probably joined the faculty by now, they'd use it as an opportunity to add a class to the curriculum about how to *not* write a novel. At least he'd be guaranteed to move some copy that way.

He could leave them to Shirley. She at least liked them... or was enough of a professional to claim that she did. That's back when she served as his champion on the front lines of the literary war and life seemed full of possibilities. Out of all those possibilities, though, it now struck him as strange that nobody stopped to consider that maybe *Dead*

Man wasn't that good, and that it sold because (a) it was decent and (b) he was tantalizingly young, the logic being that if he was a competent writer at twenty, he'd be F. Scott Fitz-fuckin'-gerald by the time he hit thirty. The possibility that he'd peaked in college never entered any conversation that he was aware of. If he gave Shirley the books, at least she would appreciate the gesture, as opposed to the hypothetical orphans, and who knows? Bequeathing the books to her might motivate her to go that extra mile, agent-wise, even though he wasn't sure what that consisted of.

Derrick pealed open a peanut butter Power Bar (at least that was flavor according to the wrapper) and absently began using it to abuse his fillings as the contemplation continued. What about Sylvia? That struck him as a strange and uncomfortable place for his mind to go… literally. Conjuring the idea generated a pinch in his guts like the onset of a bout of diarrhea. Sylvia certainly didn't deserve to have the books, based on how she treated their author, but any important decision must take into account more than a lone factor. *He* deserved to have them go to someone who knew, in some small way, what he went through in creating them. They would mean something to Sylvia, something beyond the modest income they provided. She was there, after all, during the halcyon days, and regardless of the motivations behind her presence, she… was… there.

The more he thought about it, the more it seemed right, somehow. He experienced some of the best times of his life with her (and not coincidentally, some of the worst times), and by passing the books on to her, those moments would still flicker to life in her brain every time a royalty check arrived in the mail. It wouldn't mean as much as he would like it too, but it would mean something, which was more than he could say if the books ended up with almost anyone else. Actually, thinking about it, maybe that summed up their entire relationship as much as anything: *it didn't mean as much as he would have liked it to, but it meant something, which is more than he would say about his relationship with anyone else.*

As he chewed his peanut butter Power Bar, Derrick looked out his undersized hotel window at the shockingly gloomy sky. It looked like the supernatural cloud cover at the end of the mediocre fantasy movie *Dragonslayer* that his parents took him to as a kid. Each bite required as much effort as swallowing a balloon full of heroine, which might help prepare him for his future career as a drug mule if the movie deal fell through. "Why should it fall through?" he chided himself aloud. "There's absolutely no reason to go negative this early in the process."

Pensive moments like this always provided Derrick with his most delightfully self-indulgent thoughts. He strained his neck without rising from the chair so that he could watch the people milling down on the sidewalk below, oblivious to the dragons that were no doubt on their way. There were quite a few people out in public for this early in the morning, a couple dozen that he could see, and they milled closely enough that he could make out the self-possessed looks on a few of their faces. They talked with other people, or walked assuredly on their way to someplace else or coming from someplace else. Their lives had purpose… albeit self-imposed purpose. That's what a society is: a series of social networks interconnecting. Things mean something because we all decide that they mean something: family, religion, baseball cards. Derrick felt like a dolphin among the fish, and not in a dolphins-are-smarter-than-fish kind of way. He could dip down into the water for fifteen minutes at a time, but he could never stay in that world, and he would never belong.

When you got down to it, he wasn't terribly good at being a person. He wasn't a bad person (he didn't think he was… then again, no one does), but the human condition is a mutual support system. We build bonds so that we can take turns carrying each other, depending on one's need. When you can't form those genuine bonds, you carry someone else's load when they need it, if they can con you into believing in them, but when it's your turn, you're shit out of luck. People on the outside can either look for other people on the outside to use, they can accept their role as pack mules of society, or they can just unplug from the whole mess. In this way, he supposed his worldview mimicked the one Ice Cube sang about (albeit more poetically) in "I Ain't the One."

He apparently still cared for Sylvia on some level, if thoughts of her still hurt him. This made Derrick a sap. At least most people would see him that way for having *any* concern for those who obviously had no concern for him, but the alternative was to stop caring and become what you hate, thereby violating Batman's first rule of crime-fighting. It's not weakness to withstand corruption of one's ideals; it's strength. So, even if he wasn't good at being a human, people like him were good for humanity as a whole. If serial users were pathogens of the body politic, the self-aware saps like him were like... What? Antibodies? Glial cells, maybe? Something with a protective function. Thoughts like that kept him warm at night.

A little smile had crawled across his face. He liked feeling useful. Down in his limp hand, the crinkly Power Bar wrapper sat empty. At some point in his mental wanderings, he had finished the Power Bar and would be crapping out its remains in a little less than 24 hours. He ran his index finger over the cursor pad of his laptop in order to dissolve the screen saver of his hot, auburn-tressed almost-but-not-quite-girlfriend. There were a few things he had to do today before he could start obsessing over his marathon. First, he had to log on to Etrade and see how his superconductor stocks were doing. The market was closed, but if they had crossed $25 per share, he'd have to put in a "sell" order for tomorrow. Then, he had to reply to Shirley's email.

*　　　　*　　　　*

CHAPTER THIRTEEN:
USEFUL IDIOTS

Shirley didn't hear from Derrick until the following morning, New York time. Since it was a Saturday, she read his email as she sipped her morning coffee from her home office. As usual, his message left absolutely nothing to interpretation.

Shirley:

If I die, give the rights to my books to Sylvia Sarsgaard, or whatever her name is now. If she doesn't want them, you can keep them; you've always been good to me. If the movie deal goes through, though, I bequeath them to the poorest elementary school in Camden, New Jersey.

Thanks.

Derrick

Had the message come from a normal person, Shirley might have done a spit-take with her coffee, but with Derrick, bizarre and disconnected was the norm. Her first reaction was, *Camden, New Jersey?*

Has he even been to Camden? She couldn't imagine that he had: it was a total shit hole. Upon reflection, though, that was probably the point. He probably watched a special report on *Frontline* regarding the extent of its shittiness and decided to be magnanimous.

One thing was certain: Shirley really would be sitting pretty if he did off himself, because instead of getting fifteen percent of the royalties, she'd be getting the entirety of the royalties. Throw on top of that the sales bump she expected from a newsworthy death, and she might be looking at early retirement. Since the email would be the document of legal record, though, she'd have to get an official rejection of rights from his ex-girlfriend. Thank god Derrick didn't send the message as a reply, because the agency never actually asked to get a record of rights transfer in the event of a client's death. It wouldn't do at all for the main beneficiary of his death to look like she prompted it.

And what the fuck did he mean by "you've always been good to me"? Was that some kind of joke? God knows she tried to make his life better in her agent capacity, but he was actually more successful *before* he signed with her... far more successful. Maybe he meant the cheerleading part. Her half-assed, verbal pats-on-the-back might have made him feel good enough about himself to get through the day. As far as she knew, no one ever really provided for him in the positive reinforcement department, which, of course, was the primary reason he became the standout candidate for Operation: Tortured Genius in the first place. If that's what he meant, though, she hadn't done much cheerleading in the last couple years. She just couldn't stomach the sound of her voice when she ginned up the compliments. He had plummeted from the lofty heights of *client-I-brag-about-on-airplanes* all the way down to becoming *my-main-source-of-professional-frustration*, and she couldn't hide that fact behind even her thickest layer of bullshit.

Her cat paced in the doorway, yowling to be fed. "Shut up, Pippa," Shirley absently droned from her office chair, "Mommy's working." The sound of her name caused the cat to redouble its whining. It was a cold morning, and Shirley felt contentedly stiff in her slippers and bathrobe, but she struggled to her feet before the urge to brain her cat with a half-full coffee mug overtook her. Despite the chances of an increased return on her investment, Derrick's email didn't exactly make her feel better about the situation. She'd worked to frame Derrick as a doomed loser in her mind, a man already headed down the path of offing himself in the near future, while her role was merely that of someone constructing a scenario where at least something positive would result from the disaster of his life. It didn't help Shirley to remember that he was an occasionally thoughtful doomed loser. In fact, it made her feel disgusting and vile, like the time she voted for Rudy Giuliani. She was an opportunist, almost defiantly so, but she wasn't a sociopath.

In the kitchen, she picked up the blue plastic cat food bowl and dumped a small handful of dry cat food into it. Then, she opened up a can of the Fancy Feast with the purple label and used a clean fork to scrape about a third of the can on top of the dry stuff. That slimy sound really sent Pippa into a purring frenzy. Shirley stirred the two food products together for a few seconds, before replacing the bowl next to the cat bed and checked Pippa's water dish. It was a little low and had some hairs floating in it, so she rinsed it out and fetched a bottle of water from the refrigerator.

Funny that Derrick fell for the movie lie, Shirley thought as she poured the water into the bowl. How would you even turn *Dead Man* into a decent movie? You'd have to cut out half of the parts that involved the protagonist's delusions of living in the 18th century and all the parts that were essentially pornographic. Some writers were vulnerable to those ego boosts, though, almost to the point of being blind. People don't go into writing because they're greedy; they do it because they have something to say (granted, sometimes greedy people with nothing to say become famous in other occupations, then "write" the obligatory book, but Shirley never considered them to be writers: they were egomaniacs who could type). When real writers get the opportunity to make real money, though, with no more effort on their part... hell, they're only human. On the rare occasions when that prospect came up for one of her clients in real life, she could practically see the cartoon dollar signs consume their eyeballs. Knowing Derrick, if one of his books somehow did get picked up by a movie studio, nothing would change. He'd probably still keep working in factories on the side as part of a deprivation scheme, just to make the rest of his life, the non-factory part, seem more pleasant.

On the floor, Pippa gratefully purred while simultaneously masticating the store-bought cat food. Shirley always thought Pippa was going to choke when she did that, but could cats even choke? Leaning against the counter and watching the feline version of pure joy, Shirley became cognizant of the fact that this might end up being the most pleasant part of her day.

She had to hand it to Derrick: in a weird way; he had created a strange little lifestyle off the grid, where he could subsist on virtually nothing and manage to avoid becoming a derelict. In fact, he'd probably be better off without people... like Henry Bemis in *The Twilight Zone* before he broke his glasses. People provide Derrick with a constant reflection of what he's not. She supposed that the comparison to normal lives constantly irritated him, every time he bothered to think about it. Shirley only got a glimpse of that feeling in her professional life, surrounded by the writers who had that extra one-percent of talent or luck where they could make a living off of their passions, rather than making a living off of other people's passions. The pang of disappointment now made her take off her glasses and pinch the bridge of her nose. Too early in the morning to start drowning in regret.

She replaced her glasses and took a deep breath, ready to soldier on through the remainder of her day. Unlike Derrick, she refused to passively accept the cards God had dealt her; she was fighting back in her own little way, exacting a little revenge against the fates. Life was about survival, and if people like Derrick were too stupid or weak to stand up for themselves, somebody was going to come along and take everything from them. Why shouldn't it be her?

*   *   *

Chapter Fourteen:
Slow Burn

Reginald looked down at his withered hands, as if they were a proxy for everything else wrong with him. They'd changed perceptibly over the years, but you only notice the change if you pay close attention. The loss of muscle and fat turned them wrinkled and boney. The skin on the backs of his hands looked almost transparent, and the bumps and scrapes created a constellation of scars amid the brown age spots. He had to admit, though: they looked better than they worked. At least they still looked like hands, because they sure didn't function like hands. They barely worked at all. They felt like he was wearing those thick rubber gloves that come with a new toilet brush, and they shook so bad that if he wanted to yank the tube out of his nose, he wasn't 100% sure that he could. Shooting himself in the face was a pipe dream that had faded months ago; might as well plan to pilot a rocket ship into the moon. His hands simply didn't have enough life left in them to kill him.

"Good morning, Mr. Kristoff," the day nurse said as he entered Reginald's bedroom in his light green hospital smock. Reginald wasn't sure whether he wore the nurse's uniform on the drive over or whether he changed in the bathroom. It bothered Reginald because he wanted to know what germs were being brought into his house and

into his bedroom, but he never bothered to ask.   The nurse was a good guy, and what were germs going to do? Kill him? At first Reginald thought Rick was a queer, what with his being a nurse and all… and who knows? He might have been, but that issue didn't bother Reginald any more. Rick wasn't annoyingly maudlin or optimistic and generally did what Reginald asked. He kept a tight schedule, to the extent that Reginald knew what pointless question was coming next. "How are you feeling today?"

"I want you to kill me, Rick," Reginald told him through his rasping voice that sounded like it was coming through a throat full of sand. His voice wasn't what it once was, but it was stronger than just about any other part of him; he could still call for people in the next room, and they would arrive, eventually, and he could still convince the people in his bedroom to go away. "I can't do this anymore, but I'm too damn weak to do anything about it. It's not that I don't…" He felt a tear leaking out of his eye, and the humiliation of another man seeing him cry caused what's left of his voice to crack and crumble. "I—I just can't do it anymore."

To his credit, Rick didn't freak out. He stayed professional, grabbing a Kleenex and leaning forward, just in case Reginald started snotting. Maybe this wasn't the first time Rick heard this request. Maybe it wasn't the first time this week. That was his job: carrying people across the finish line, and some people needed more help than others. "It's okay, Mr. Kristoff. Just talk to me."

*   *   *

Paradoxically, the first few miles of the race were typically the toughest for Derrick. Marathon running is all about establishing a pace and a rhythm. Derrick's larger than normal body took longer than normal to establish that rhythm. Starting out, everything feels awkward and slow, like your legs are being operated by a hand crank. You start breathing hard way too early. Within a few miles, you catch a bounce to your step, and running actually feels good for ten minutes or so, but then the joint and muscle aches creep in. You try to stretch or adjust, but that's like jamming your fingers into the proverbial leaking dike: as soon as one problem gets addressed, two more spring into existence. A few more miles, and the minor aches get chased away by the endorphin rush and the numbness. After that, it's smooth sailing… for a few miles, but then your lungs start burning and your heart starts pounding so hard you start to hear a pinging sound, like microscopic hobgoblins striking your eardrum with a ball peen hammer. The last few miles are a battle that really doesn't have a script, but the point is, if you can't establish a rhythm in those first few miles, you might not even last long enough to worry about all that other stuff.

Finding the necessary rhythm. Derrick always considered that as an appropriate running metaphor for his life. He performed optimally when his day-to-day behaviors remained on autopilot, where everything was practiced and routine and he didn't have to think in order to get stuff done. Everything just seemed to happen automatically and without drama. It allowed for him to save his energy and resources for the dramatic breaks from routine (e.g., quitting his job and jetting off to East Asia) that also peppered his biography.

He liked that metaphor, and it fit his life nicely, but then he ran a race in the high plains desert of Wyoming where he found an even better one. The race route forced runners to spend about ten miles above 7,500 feet and, between the incline and the elevation, Derrick got exhausted halfway through. He felt weak as a kitten and his vision was a tad blurry, but he also didn't want to spend four hours hobbling along above the cloud-line in August. So, he decided to walk/run the last thirteen miles to the finish line. The race took place on a dusty horse trail, so Derrick intermittently used the piles of horse turds on the road as focal points to where he could stop running and start walking again. The last half of the race literally involved running from one pile of shit to the next. That turned out to be an even better metaphor for his life.

Derrick thought about these things as the start gun sounded and he and about 25,000 other mediocre runners crept toward the start line in a wave of Rayon-clad humanity. At 6'1", he could see the tops of thousands of raven-tressed heads. He liked his chances of getting a good time, not because he trained especially hard during the lead-up to the race, but because he took an especially big dump in the subway station bathroom under Gwanghwamun Plaza. When you eat a bunch of carbs the day before a run, it's going to come out at some point. So, you have to time your food consumption so that you make your space in your digestive tract for when the food you ate the night before comes creeping down your small intestine. Otherwise, a big dump in the middle of a race destroys your rhythm. It slows you down, causes cramps, and otherwise disrupts a perfectly good run. This problem continued to bedevil Derrick, in part because that pharmaceutical-grade opium that he ingested constipated him and made everything irregular. That's why, even though the race started at 8:30 a.m., Derrick woke up at six to drink two cups of coffee. That got the elimination process started off right, and he shuffled to the start line feeling confident and light.

Other factors aligned in his favor. The morning was cool, probably in the mid-forties, if he performed the correct Celsius-to-Fahrenheit conversions. The crisp air made the pre-race preparations a little painful on his exposed epidermis, but staying in the mass of humanity minimized the wind chill, and once he got moving, that temperature would become ideal. The air seemed reasonably clean, what with the slight breeze blowing out of the west and the minimal Sunday morning traffic from the major streets getting blocked off for the race. Air quality wasn't something you had to worry about in rural Wyoming, but in East Asia, it was just a fact of life. He just hoped that the Koreans in the race didn't run like they did everything else (i.e., intrusively). He already knew how to say excuse me in Korean, but after a few dozen people cut him off, he'd start wishing he had cracked open his travel book before he left the hotel and learned how to shout, "Are you fucking blind?!"

The race organizers staggered the start of the race based on expected time, which placed Derrick back with the 3:30 people. A relatively eclectic group. A healthy number of toned women clad in black tights and running shorts, along with a few obvious foreigners. The group populations got more and more homogenous (i.e., Korean) the further back in the pack you got; you don't spend the time and money traveling to Seoul for a marathon if you *totally* suck.

The time for the 3:30 group to start running had nearly arrived, and a halting creep toward the start line for people in that group turned into a stalk. Derrick walked briskly, over-striding to stretch out his hamstrings. The computer chip attached to his shoelaces would keep his official time, and it wouldn't start until he crossed the orange rubber mat that served as the start line. He felt alert, kinetic even. Nothing had excited him in a long time, which magnified his current state (the possibility of the movie deal didn't count, because he still didn't quite believe it; he treated it the same way he would a carnival gypsy telling him that he was going to be president). His heart beat steadily in his chest, but strongly enough for him to feel it. The crowd cheered just as incoherently as an American crowd and banged those horribly annoying, inflatable plastic sticks together. More than anything, Derrick felt alive, unlike he had during the almost four months that had elapsed since he ran in Las Vegas.

He heard a light, electronic beep as he stepped on the orange rubber and began to run. *Run like T-Rex* he told himself and lifted his hands and tucked his elbows in. *Chin down, flat back*, he thought and forced his shoulders back. He repeated the mantras several times in the initial moments of the race. During the first couple miles, the better your form, the less energy you waste and the faster you can establish a rhythm. Eventually, his thoughts would drift to completely unrelated issues, but he would find himself repeating, "Chin down, flat back," dozens of times before he crossed the finish line. Toward the end of the race, he would say it aloud to himself.

Unlike most modern runners, Derrick never ran with an iPod or other listening device. He had no doubt about its entertainment value or the fact that it helped pass the time, but he avoided them for three reasons. First, from a practical standpoint, it struck him as irresponsible and a little dangerous. If you can't hear, you're more likely to shift over and run into people trying to pass you. Plus, he'd seen people trying to fuck with their iPod when it wasn't working properly and almost crash into a fellow runner; he didn't want to be That Guy. Plus, he'd had instances where he was so wiped out at the end of a long run that he could barely see, and only his keen hearing kept him from walking into the path of a pizza delivery truck. Second, from a philosophical standpoint he considered overstimulation to be one of the major problems of the modern world. People in modern society couldn't focus because they couldn't live without constant stimulation; it's why so many kids had ADHD (no, he didn't believe in the bullshit food-dye hypothesis). He didn't want to fall into that pattern of needing it to function. The sights and sounds and smells of central Seoul would have to entertain him. Finally, and most obviously, Derrick didn't want to pass the time. He didn't fly halfway around the world to casually burn calories and wait for it to be over; he wanted to remember every single painful, monotonous step for as long as humanly possible. He didn't get to feel truly alive very often, and he wasn't about to waste this opportunity.

*   *   *

Derrick staggered into his hotel room, absently deciding whether to simply drop his dirty, salt-caked body onto the bed or to go through the contortions of taking a shower first. Ultimately, his compulsive nature overrode his fatigue and he decided to grunt his way through a shower. Every gross-motor movement... lifting his foot to step into the shower, twisting, the shower dial, reaching for the soap... sent a bolt of pain shooting through him, but it was worth it; washing all the shit from the race off of himself felt like being born. The water splashed over him, and he could taste the salt crystals when a little bit of the spray ended up in his mouth. Besides the disgusting film on his skin, he had the horrific hip and shoulder pain and muscle soreness to deal with it. The shower jet massaged some of it away, and a couple Aleve would help, but it would take a few days for the aches to fully subside. With his shower complete, he gingerly walked out of the bathroom with a white hotel bath towel wrapped around his waist and collapsed face-first onto the invisibly stained comforter, thus ending one of the most physically challenging ordeals of his life. Not the race... that part was fairly typical; the hardest part was getting home.

As always, as soon as he stepped across the marathon finish line, Derrick felt like he had walked away from a car accident. This time was actually a little worse than normal, so bad that he had to flop backward onto the infield of the Olympic Stadium and let his lungs start absorbing oxygen again. He blamed it on his track instincts kicking in during that last 200 meters and causing a sprint to the finish. Layers of clouds still clung to the sky and formed a lampshade for the sun. Staring up at the heavens, spent lungs heaving, Derrick wondered if a steroid-addled Ben

Johnson felt this way after he blew past Carl Lewis all those years ago. He

doubted it. Sprinting tires you out in a different way; it feels more like

finishing a tough workout instead of wringing out your body and soul like

a dirty rag. After little more than a minute, before his joints could lock

up, he climbed to his feet again. Staggering over to the refreshment tent,

he picked up a couple bottles of water and a plain bagel from two women

wearing oversized, completely superfluous sun visors. His murky, post-

race stomach wouldn't be able accept food for at least an hour, but by

that time, he'd be hungry enough to chew off his arm. As it turned out,

that hour would pass before he even returned to the hotel.

Derrick thought he had considered every eventuality before he

set out on his run. He put his hotel keycard and about fifty dollars in

Korean currency into a money belt and clipped it around his waist. Fifty

thousand Korean won would probably buy him cab rides to the hotel, the

train station, and then the airport, but he wanted to be sure. Everything

stayed in place throughout the run, and even if the money was still a little

soggy, in 40 degree weather, it would surely dry out in matter of minutes.

Now, unfortunately, even as he slowly wandered past the little picnic

camps of Koreans and the putrid smell of their fermented cabbage boiling

away in little hot pots, he couldn't find the subway station for the

Olympic Park. He didn't want to roam too far, because that would

require roaming back, and his body hurt far too badly for bipedal

experimentation. Also, his language limitations prevented him from (a)

asking for directions or (b) understanding those directions had anyone

offered them. Although he did bring more than enough (soggy) money to

pay for a cab ride back to the hotel, that plan required cab drivers to

actually stop and pick up his poor, disheveled, sweaty ass, which didn't happen. He wondered if *that* decision had anything to do with the purported cock-size of foreigners.

Feeling naked and alone, with no other options available, he started his stiff and painful walk back toward the middle of the city. Every shift of his joints sent a jolt through his system. It was an algorithmic plan: just walk toward the big buildings. He knew very little about the Seoul subways system, but from his experience in New York City, he knew that if he walked long enough and stuck to main thoroughfares, he would eventually find a subway station. Unfortunately, he ended up on the long end of "eventually." By the time he marched across a high concrete bridge that spanned a sizeable river, it became apparent that the ideal temperature for running twenty-six miles was not ideal for slowly walking in a sweat-soaked T-shirt and running shorts. The river acted like a natural funnel for cold, fast-moving air as it enveloped his exposed flesh. Walking east from the Olympic Park, it took over twenty minutes of labored walking and constant shivering before he found a subway station. Due to his sweaty money and blurred vision, it took another ten minutes to buy the correct ticket from the vending machine. Ticket in hand, staring at the foggy map, he calculated that he would need to endure thirteen stops and two transfers to make it back to the hotel.

It felt like a late-night, forced march home after binge-drinking: the simplest behaviors (e.g., walking, staying awake, not puking) took all of his effort and focus. Only after Derrick finally commandeered a subway seat next to an old Korean woman with a two-wheeled grocery cart did he give himself even odds of being able to keep from throwing up before he passed out. Although part of him was curious as to what his body *could* throw up at that point, he badly wanted to avoid any variety of physical collapse. Besides the obvious pain and humiliation, he feared creating a salient, negative stereotype of Americans for about one hundred onlookers and to whomever they told the story. Some would excuse him because he still wore his running number pinned to the front of his shirt, but for others, he would provide living proof of how undisciplined and socially irresponsible Americans were… and even though, in his experience, Americans did tend to be undisciplined and socially irresponsible, he didn't want to carry the weight of being the person who created or sustained that belief, because it might make the world a slightly worse place for some poor English teacher who followed him.

These thoughts ran through his head as he wrapped his thin, shaking arms around his torso, pressed his elbows against his knees, stared at the floor, and tried to count the subway station stops. He tried counting the seconds between stops, but it was hard to focus for more than thirty seconds at a time. For the moment, the station stops were his piles of horse turds in the desert, beckoning in the distance, leading him to safety. Mantra's wouldn't help (his chin was down, but his back wasn't straight), and metaphors featuring poop aren't that useful when you're nauseous, but he still had his life philosophies to keep his focus, to drive him onward through the fatigue. *Don't be an ugly American,* he told himself. It was a common theme. If he had picked just one clichéd affirmation to lock onto above all others to get him through difficult situations, it would be "first, do no harm." Actually, that's not true, either; it would be "always wipe and stay off the pipe," but the doctor one would be a close second.

*   *   *

CHAPTER FIFTEEN:

BRIDE OF THE SPACE MAN

"They've put together an office pool about how long you've got left in your office," Samantha told Shirley out on the smoking balcony. Her smoke and words quickly disappeared into the wind rushing down Fourth Avenue. "I wouldn't take it personally; everybody's worried about their own... tenuous position, so they focus on someone else's. I just thought you should know."

Shirley considered asking who "they" were, but the answer was either "everyone in the office" or "nearly everyone in the office." She and Samantha had been having such a nice conversation about fichus plants when Samantha tossed that one at her from left field and beaned Shirley in the head. Sam seemed preoccupied throughout the conversation, but Shirley only noticed it in retrospect. She certainly never thought Sam's preoccupation applied to *her*. "Well, I assume that at least some people are betting long," she said with a glint of uncharacteristic optimism. The morning chill seemed to dramatically deepen in a matter of seconds, and she gripped the neck of her coat closed with her ungloved hand.

Samantha turned her head away from the wind and blew a slow stream of smoke through her pursed lips like an aged 1950's starlet. She was one of the few people Shirley knew who smoked like she was proud of it. Most people smoked with posture of inmates in a prison yard, but there was no hunching over or directionally exhaling for Sam. She summoned forth air from her tar-caked lungs like it smelled of honeysuckle and roses. Her husband smoked high-end cigars, so maybe tobacco fetishism formed part of their self-image as a couple. "That's only because the recent slots were the first ones to fill up," she replied with her characteristic casual wit.

"Wow. So, it's an actual pool," Shirley said, smoking her own cigarette more aggressively, "with slots and whatnot." She shook her head, exasperated. "I suppose that no one cares that slumps happen all the time when you sign clients to multi-book deals. It makes it look like you haven't done anything in a while until they need that new contract. It's a cycle."

Samantha made a sucking sound as she pulled the Capri away from her lips. "If that was an actual question, than no, no one cares." Before Shirley could do any more than inhale another hit, Samantha quickly clarified. "They *should* care, because they know that's how this business works sometimes, and it could be their sorry ass in the same position next year, but we both know print is in trouble, and if the agency's going to make themselves look fiscally responsible, they can't exactly dump someone who just signed a client to a five-book deal. They have to do it to someone in a slump." She took another pull, looking calm and above the fray. She could afford to; when you're husband's a CPA, the worst-case scenario ain't all that bad. "Have you talked with your film contacts?"

"I'm really not plugged in there," Shirley admitted, feeling more fidgety with each passing minute. The self-help book about de-stressing that she was reading said that conversation with friends was supposed to *calm* you. Maybe she needed new friends. Maybe she was going to have to make some new ones (i.e., after she got fired), whether she wanted to or not. "I've had so many times where I had something rock-solid and it fell through at the last minute." Her recently plucked eyebrows arched. "'Rock-solid.' Their words, not mine. It got so frustrating that I had to stop dealing with that industry unless they approached me. Just for my health, y'know?"

Samantha nodded and they both took synchronized drags on their cigarettes. "I know what you mean, doll. It's so impersonal over there. Everybody's on the make, doesn't have time to cultivate real relationships." She shook her head. "Some of those head-cases are just as bad as clients... just talking with them ages you. And then you have to turn around and tell the client the bad news. The look on their faces is like when you tell your kids that there's no Santa Claus."

Shirley nodded as though she empathized, but they both knew Samantha had two more kids than Shirley ever would have. The fact never bothered her in her thirties, not even a little, but she wasn't in her thirties anymore. Mother's Day lingered a couple months away... that wouldn't be pleasant. "How long do you give me?" she asked, as if Samantha was her oncologist.

"At least a month," Samantha said, trying to sound hopeful, obviously already having given it some thought. One month. In publishing, that's about how long it took them to come up with a font for the cover.

"Seriously?" Shirley said, grinding out the smoldering stub of her cigarette on the concrete ledge. "It's that bad?"

"I don't know," Samantha admitted, but she would have said the same thing even if she did know. "I don't have access to the company books and I can't read Roger's mind. I don't know if they have to fire someone, but if they start cleaning house, which I think they will, I would guess your number would be up. You never were one of Roger's favorites in the first place."

"I should have offered to sleep with him," Shirley said, ruefully thinking aloud, "back when that mattered." Her mind kept churning to the obvious conclusion: *Back when he would have said "yes."* Samantha didn't answer. She just kept looking out in the general direction of the Hudson. "You didn't… join the pool, did you?"

Samantha shrugged without turning. "It was only five bucks."

*   *   *

"Hello?" Shirley said into the mouthpiece of her office phone. "Ms. Sarsgaard?"

"It's Mrs. Nelson now, but this is her," the voice on the other end of the line said. The tone was clipped, like she'd woken up with a migraine. Shirley tried to place the accent, but never did that very well with non-New York people.

"Mrs. Nelson," Shirley tried again, using the side of her skull to pin the receiver to her shoulder as she wrote down "Nelson" on her pad of Post-It Notes. It was a practiced move. Would handless phone-holding become a lost art, what with cellular phones being so small? She wondered. "My name is Shirley Martin, I'm Derrick Kessler's literary agent." Privately, she added, *for the near future, at least… one way or another.*

"Oh Jesus Christ," Sylvia muttered on the other end. "What is it this time? He trashed my likeness in a book and needs my permission? Because that's not happening for less than a thousand dollars."

"Nothing like that," Shirley assured her, neglecting to mention that (1) a libel conviction would get you a hell of a lot more than a thousand bucks and (2) a libel complaint about a fictional likeness would get thrown out of court in about two seconds. Out of curiosity, she asked, "Has he contacted you recently?"

"What? No. I haven't talked to him in, like, six years," Sylvia said, sharply. This broad seemed like a real treat to deal with on a daily basis. Once the compliments run dry, you're probably just catching a lot of fire and ice. "I just always half expect to, though. Derrick never could let go of things. He has this whole... complex."

"Uh-huh," Shirley said, sort of understanding, but not really. She leaned back in her office chair, stretching the coiled phone cord. Derrick did have a hard time letting things go, despite his best efforts, but the main thing he had trouble letting go of was the two-ton ball of guilt he kept shackled to his neck. He didn't like to "inflict himself on other people" (his words... or at least the words of one of his more transparent autobiographical characters from a recent book). Such being the case, Shirley doubted he would contact Sylvia, after all this time, out of fear of disrupting her life. A couple seconds passed, punctuated by light breathing, before Shirley remembered that it was her turn to advance the conversation. "Um, the reason I'm contacting you is because Derrick specified that in the event of his death, he wants his literary property rights to get transferred to you."

"Oh," Sylvia said, sounding slightly surprised. Her tone brightened at the prospect of getting that thousand dollars, after all. "Okay. Yeah, that's fine. What's it worth?"

Shirley bristled and put the finishing touches on her primordial opinion that Sylvia must be a massive bitch. Maybe it's because she was a cog in the literary machine, but Shirley had a clear appreciation of how much these stupid little books individually (much less collectively) mean to the people who write them. For some, a book was like a Frankenstein monster assembled from some unholy combination of the writer's children and everlasting soul, but to this little cunt, receiving the rights to someone's book was about as emotionally evocative as getting a letter from the government indicating that they had screwed up her tax return.

"After advances are covered, it's, um, royalty-based, which means that it's dependent on a percentage of the volume of overall sales, so I really can't project how much it will be worth by the time, and if, you receive them."

She could practically hear Sylvia shrugging on the other end of the line. "So, do I just have to sign something?"

Shirley kept expecting her to ask if Derrick was alright, but the question never came. Over the course of their mercifully brief conversation, it became clear which female character Derrick based on Sylvia: the girlfriend from *Ham-Handed*. She couldn't remember the character's name (it wasn't "Sylvia," or even "Silvia"), but she was a hyper-feminist hippy chick when it was fashionable in college who married a banker and started voting Republican and shooting out babies before she hit twenty-five. That character didn't deserve to own the rights to Derrick's manuscripts, so of course, neither did Sylvia. She'd wandered too far down into her own web of lies to back out now, but at least Shirley could inconvenience the little bitch. "There's only a single form," she said, "and the only issue is that you'll have to come to New York to sign the copyright transfer."

"Why do I have to sign it in person?" Sylvia whined, suddenly finding the gift decidedly inconvenient. "You can't just fax it to me or send it as an email attachment and I can mail it back?"

"No, because it has to be notarized," Shirley lied.

"Jesus," Sylvia said in a voice Shirley often heard used by people (usually children) trying to wear down the other side with their whininess. Little did she know that Shirley responded to that tonal shift like a call-to-arms. "It's not like he wrote *The Davinci Code*."

"Yeah," Shirley said, trying to sound sympathetic, "I don't even know why we even need the consent of the receiver… or why it can't be something that's transferred through a normal will and testament. It's something that only happens with patents and copyrights. I don't know. I'm not a lawyer."

"Obviously," Sylvia snorted, although Shirley had no idea what was so obvious about it. They do have lawyers at the firm; contracts need to be written, after all, but they hire people like Shirley for their knowledge of verb tense and their winning charm. "How long do I have to decide?"

"There's no real finite time-limit," Shirley explained, then added, "until he becomes incapacitated… or changes his mind."

"He's not like, terminally ill or anything, though, right?" That was the closest that Sylvia came to voicing any sort of concern about her former boyfriend, but it mostly served to assess the urgency of the situation. If it wasn't a pressing issue, she could always swing up north during the family vacation to Cooperstown.

"Not that I'm aware of," Shirley said, smiling mirthlessly into the phone.

"Well, I'll let you know if I'm going to be in New York in the near future," Sylvia offered. "Is your number… 212-555-8264?"

"That's the one" Shirley said. "Where do you live, by the by?"

"Virginia. North of Richmond."

"Wow. That *is* a trip," Shirley said, and refrained from adding, *A three-hour trip.* Instead, she gave the little bitch her name and email, and they exchanged remarkably pleasant goodbyes.

As was usually the case when meeting a client's current or former main squeeze, Shirley couldn't help but try to imagine what the couple acted like in private together. Sylvia seemed a little too pushy for someone like Derrick to effectively tolerate, but he was nothing if not a masochist. Maybe when she shifted into bitch-mode, he thought he deserved it. Maybe her sex appeal, nearly invisible in a phone conversation, overwhelmed the rational part of his brain. Maybe it was like the old Bob Seger song, and she could turn on the charm long enough to get her by. All Shirley knew was that it would be a damn shame if Derrick offed himself, those books started selling, and all the money got sucked up by some ingrate in Bump Ass, Virginia.

Shirley wrote Derrick an email and sent it before she left work, telling him that the studio called and said they were trying to line up a director for *Dead Man: The Movie.* Did he want her to try to get him a screenwriter credit? She didn't enjoy writing or sending that email; the Sylvia incident made her lies feel less clever, but she stomached the distaste and soldiered on. It was a dog-eat-dog world, and if the dirty feeling didn't go away, she could always take an extra shower when she got home.

*   *   *

CHAPTER SIXTEEN:
RIGHTEOUS JEWS

Harry walked briskly through the relentless drizzle, rolled up newspaper tucked under his arm, tubular parcel wedged inside the newspaper. The non-descript, black umbrella arching overhead would protect the newspaper from getting too wet, but when he placed it in the rubbish bin, it would have less than a minute before the rain soaked through the newspaper. Timing was everything in this business, even for a simple handoff. He thought it stupid at the time, when trainers at the Agency spent hours teaching him how to walk in a manner where he looked self-possessed, but at the same time made sure that his steps fell in rhythm with a metronome. They did this with everybody, and the payoff became obvious once you entered the field. On the one hand, it made the covert operatives blend in to the sea of oblivious civilians and harder to detect. On the other hand, it made everyone's movements fit together like the gears of a handcrafted watch.

As Harry approached the intersection, the traffic light on the other side of the street signaled for pedestrians to walk. He stepped off the curb and the rubber soles of his shoes slapped the pavement in a rhythmic pattern. Along the way, he drifted half-a-step over to his right, toward the rubbish bin near the entrance to the pub, and without meaning to, he spotted his contact. A round-shouldered man wearing a bowler and no umbrella… just a tick less than two meters tall. Certainly, no one at the Agency had taken the time to train him to appear inconspicuous. He milled about, looked for all the world like the inept, secondary henchman of a James Bond villain. Regardless, once Harry let go of the parcel and dropped it amongst the papers and cans and god-knows-what-else, his role in this game would (finally) be finished. He shifted the newspaper from his left arm to his right, but before he could let it go, he felt the unmistakable sensation of a gun barrel pressing into his ribs. They never taught him the meaning of that sensation at the agency; they didn't have to. "There's a good lad," a man's voice in his ear hissed. "Keep on walking straight away."

They continued their methodical march across the street, reaching the other side right ahead of the changing traffic light. The intended recipient of the package had his back turned, lighting (or pretending to light) a cigarette, and they strolled right on by. When the rounded man turned back, he would probably spend a pair of minutes digging through the trash, fuming, and they would be long gone. Timing, once again, was everything… especially for the big things. Harry felt the newspaper slowly sliding out from the crook of his arm, backward toward the gunman. "Now, you're going to keep walking for another thirty seconds. If you turn around before thirty seconds, one of your fellow pedestrians is going to shoot you in the head. Are we clear?"

"If I don't try to stop you, I'll be dead in sixty seconds," Harry remarked, somewhat hopelessly. Going the sympathetic route may not have been the best idea, but no doubt, Harry was reminding this fellow, not telling him something he didn't know.

"On the contrary, I expect that your employer anticipated this on some level," the man said as they continued their synchronized walk. He said it in an assuring tone, as if he just wanted what was best for everyone. "When they ask you what happened, tell them that you were relieved of your clandestine duties by Rick Shaw."

"Rick Shaw?" Harry repeated. He'd heard the name before, of course, in espionage circles it gets bandied about, but he thought the name was used to refer to an unknown entity, like John Doe, except that the unknown entity was malevolent.

Unless this fellow was in on the joke, that meant he had a lot of trouble to answer for. When Harry didn't get an answer, he nearly glanced over his shoulder and probably would have caught a bullet in the head from one of the black-clad buggers stalking north or south. Instead, he kept his chin in his chest and marched to the end of the block, where he would wait for the rounded man to arrive and start yelling at him. As long as he didn't get executed, he would be happy to leave this stage of the game. It had gotten way too serious since he stepped off the curb.

*   *   *

As Derrick sat at the corner table of the Dunkin' Doughnuts down the street from his hotel, his laptop positioned in front of him, he contemplated the best and worst days of his life. His half cup of coffee had stopped steaming moments ago and would grow cold a few moments hence. He was a borderline-compulsive list-maker, and so, on this day, with so much fundamental change lingering in the air, he decided to open a new window in Microsoft Word and make it a "Top Five" and a "Bottom Five" list for "Days of My Life." For some strange reason, he found the bottom five days a lot easier to generate. As for the top five, the day he published *Dead Man* was up there, of course; he never came so close to mattering as he did that day. The other options, though, were the sort of days that seemed good at the time, but ended up being a delusion or a flat-out lie... like the first time he slept with Sylvia. Did it still count as a good day if the moment made him initially happy but got warped and perverted over time into something painful and scarring, thereby poisoning future days? He supposed not; it would be like labeling the day the atomic bomb was dropped as a proud day in his nation's history. If he didn't count those types of days, though, he had to scrape to come up with five. In any event, he decided to include that very day on the list of the Top Five... even though it had just started.

Perhaps it came from the post-race endorphin rush, perhaps from a recognizable contrast to the constant *blah* his life had become for the preceding three months, but Derrick awoke feeling more spry than he had in weeks, and things only got better after checking the ol' email inbox. The mystery studio had begun the process of picking a mystery director. While that struck him as surprisingly fast, the decision should make the internet news, so that even if the movie didn't actually get made, it would still bump up sales of *Dead Man*, slightly, and maybe even some of the other one's (except *Thanatos*... he wasn't sure it was even still in print). This series of events meant that Derrick's life wouldn't get markedly worse for the near future, which, for someone who tried to live in the moment, was about as much as he could ask for. It seemed like time to relax and accept that something good had happened.

He just wanted to be happy, and although that might be the most unabashedly trite expression in the history of the English language, for him, it held a particular specificity. Derrick didn't believe in God. He didn't believe in life after death, either. Or that he would ever get married or have kids or do anything terribly consequential before his death, an event which, as someone who lived in the moment, he continually expected to happen in the next twenty-four hours. He still hoped for all of these things to varying degrees, he just didn't honestly see them as realistic outcomes to his life. This left him with a pair of maxims that he had to follow in order to sleep at night: (1) first, do no harm, and (2) try to be happy. With the way humans were fucking the planet, he didn't believe mankind would survive the next fifty years, so all facets of existence lacked permanence, but with permanence as a relative concept, he'd rationalized that each moment of his life contained as much value as any other moment of any other life. So, while this philosophy saw big victories as inherently unattainable, by trying to be happy and trying not to be a douchebag, he could manage to win a series of small victories on a daily basis. He tried to articulate all this in his unpublished manuscript, *Edifice Complex*, but it got too preachy too quick, and he didn't need Shirley to tell him that no publisher would want to inflict his particular brand of existential angst onto its readers.

That was his real limitation as a writer: he couldn't effectively convey any depth into his stories without it descending into self-indulgent moping or boasting. He could construct a decent plot. He could create realistic characters, and he could get them to engage in brisk dialogue. His action sequences stayed lean and mean and his resolutions often both surprised and satisfied. He was, at worst, a serviceable writer and, at best, a good one. He would never be great, though, until he could tell a story so beautiful that it directly resulted in someone openly weeping, and you can't do that when you're self-obsessed. In all probability, Rick Shaw's ambiguous saga would not provide a vehicle to that transcendent place, but he didn't know what else would, either.

Think happy thoughts, he reminded himself as he clicked back over to the window containing his nearly two pages of a story where Rick Shaw is a master spy… for some reason, *or this day is going to drop right out of the Top Five.*

*   *   *

Derrick brought up the topic of his literary Achilles heel with Phillip at a celebratory coffee later that evening (after a series of emails to schedule the event). Phillip listened with that perpetual smile on his face that made Derrick wonder if he was genuinely happy or merely amused. "What a wonderful dilemma to have," he said when Derrick finished talking.

Derrick flinched, like someone had flicked his nose, and immediately, he found something about the surface of the table very interesting. "Well, I mean, I know that there are a lot of people who have it worse —"

"What?" Phillip said, his smile falling away for a moment. He kept both hands wrapped around his coffee. That's how he drank coffee, like he was forcing the heat back into the cup. "Oh, no, no. I didn't mean it in a 'luxury of the privileged' kind of way. I just mean that it's admirable to aspire to greatness. It is a low-percentage endeavor, but more people should at least attempt it. The world would be a much better place."

The words hung in the air for a few seconds as Derrick tried to digest them. Their implication was *exactly* the sort of thing he wanted to hear, so looked for ways to fend off the compliment. "I don't know, man," Derrick said. "Hitler aspired to greatness." He got a lot out of talking to Phillip. In a way, it was his ideal interpersonal relationship: interesting, intellectual, and temporary.

"And the sheep that followed him did not," Phillip immediately countered. He'd probably anticipated Derrick's insight. In order to define the polls of morality in Western culture, one has to consider how they apply to Jesus and Hitler. WWHD?

Derrick sipped his coffee out of the white porcelain mug as he contemplated a response. He didn't sip in order to savor; he sipped because the coffee tasted like ass. This coffee shop (named "Da Vinci's," for some reason), like most Korean cafés, didn't served "brewed coffee." They only used had espresso machines, so the closest approximation of a real cup of coffee was a Café Americano, which Derrick considered the equivalent of a person drinking regular coffee and having diarrhea into a cup. That's why he wanted to go to Dunkin' Doughnuts... again, but Phillip hated the hard wooden chairs there, so they met at this place. Admittedly, the plush booths were cushier than the chairs at Dunkin'

Doughnuts, but you don't go to a coffee shop for the chairs, just like you don't go to the movies for the popcorn. Finally, after another second bitter sip, Derrick said. "That's an interesting point. I just have a hard time believing that the world would be a better place with more dysfunctional people like me in it."

Phillip's eyes widened. "What are you talking about? Of course it would. Are you joking?"

Derrick gazed down at his dark reflection in the coffee. Another compliment. Two in one day. He didn't know how to take criticism from others, but he never felt especially bad about that because he also didn't know how to take compliments. It kind of evened out in the end. Are you supposed to say thank you? That always felt like cheapening the moment. Are you supposed to be modest and try to deny them, even in the instances when you agree? He usually settled for looking horribly uncomfortable. In this case, he didn't remotely believe the compliment. A world with more self-absorbed neurotics like him seemed like a depressing (albeit thinner) place. "What makes you say that?" he asked without looking up.

Phillip's response was immediate, like he'd been preparing the entire time Derrick spent staring into his coffee. "Most evil in the world is perpetuated by the stupid and the weak," Phillip said, counting off the pair of attributes on his right hand. Then, he switched hands. "Whatever else you are, you are smart and disciplined. So, even if you never become a 'great' writer, you are making the world a better place by making it slightly easier for others to be smart and disciplined. We are less outnumbered."

"We?" Derrick said, looking up.

"The smart and disciplined people," Phillip clarified, straightening in his chair. He carried himself in such a way that he looked taller than

Derrick, even though he was several inches shorter. "Yes," he continued, after a slight pause, "unlike you, I have no problem considering myself smart and disciplined."

"So, mere existence is enough? Existence justifies itself?"

"Well, consider: if you merely exist, you probably aren't that smart or disciplined," Phillip countered. "Those attributes require work."

"Wow," Derrick said, genuinely impressed. "You certainly have thought this through."

"I was a Religious Studies major as an undergraduate," Phillip said, taking a sip of whatever the hell frothy crap he ordered. "Vanderbilt University. Go Commodores," he said, half-heartedly pumping his fist for effect.

Derrick's face squeezed itself quizzical. "There's a religion that revolves around that concept?"

"No, not that 'revolve around it,'" Phillip said, making a quick circle with his index finger. "They all feature it, but, in my humble opinion, don't emphasize it enough. For instance, are you familiar with the concept of the tsadakim?"

"Probably not," Derrick admitted. He found religion interesting, but mostly in an isn't-that-stupid kind of way. He got a kick out of the stories about magical underwear, boycotts of ham, and the like. He never liked it to the point where he explored the philosophical underpinnings of specific religions, but that's why god created Religious Studies majors.

"Well," Phillip began, "it's the concept that there are thirty-seven people... righteous men... whose presence keeps the world from being destroyed."

"Like the Justice League?" Derrick asked, half in jest. Strangely, Phillip knew the reference, but he didn't catch the minor attempt at humor. "That's more like personal intervention by demigods," he explained. "What I am referring to is more like the idea that God is kept from intervening… in an Old Testament kind of way… by the presence of these people."

Derrick scratched at his eyebrow. Behind him, the Korean barista screeched and waved her hands in excitement at the appearance of a pair of familiar customers in her doorway. No doubt a conversation in their indecipherable moon-language would ensue. Trying to regain his train of thought, Derrick offered, "So they… don't like God?"

Phillip shook his head, but his grin reappeared. "I'm explaining this poorly." He paused, thinking. "Okay, you know the story of Sodom and Gomorrah and their destruction?"

"Sure," Derrick said, even though that the version of the tale that sprung into his head when Phillip mentioned the twin cities was from a hilarious *Super Deluxe* cartoon he saw on YouTube that depicted the event in a manner that was hyper-sexualized, oversimplified, and poorly drawn. "Lot's wife turning into a pillar of salt and whatnot."

"Well, Lot was the righteous man who kept those cities from being destroyed, and he was told by angels to leave the cities so that they would be devoid of righteous individuals and God could then destroy it."

"Why didn't God just move him?"

Phillip stared at him for a couple seconds, maybe to gage his seriousness. "You know that's not how it works. God doesn't teleport people across space."

Derrick nodded. He was acting like a bit of a dick, sidetracking Phillip with his random questions, so he didn't bother asking why God didn't destroy the city that Lot didn't live in (Gomorrah?) as a warning to the other city. Sure, it was a legitimate point, but you could spend all day questioning the logic of fables. "So, why are there thirty-seven of these people?"

"The number is rather arbitrary," Phillip explained. "You have to remember that the Old Testament involved a rather small proportion of people on the planet. Perhaps the specific number has some significance in ancient Hebrew numerology."

"I wonder if the number stays constant, even though there are so many more people now." Behind him, the Koreans patrons were yapping loudly with the barista and flipping through an art catalogue that had materialized on the counter. Since none of them said "hello," "thank you," or "toilet," Derrick had no idea what the conversation entailed.

"I would guess not," Phillip offered. "Again, the exact number is not important."

"So, do you believe in that story?"

"Not *exactly* that story," Phillip said. "I'm not certain that I believe in God, much less the Hebrew God. Given what we know now, the specifics of the stories from the Old Testaments are rather quaint: God created the entire world… the entire *universe*… but was only concerned about a tiny section of the Middle East?" He removed his hands from his mug long enough to hold them up in a silent, questioning pose. "That seems so… local. I'm just fascinated by the tsadakim as a concept in and of itself: there are righteous people in the world who keep it intact, and their number isn't important, beyond the idea that the more plentiful they are, the better off we all are."

"So, do you think that you and I are tsadakim?" Derrick asked in his inimitable blunt style, probably mispronouncing the operative word. With unfamiliar words, it was hard to tell whether the sound came from the way Phillip spoke or the actual pronunciation.

"No," Phillip said, obviously disappointed in Derrick. "I told you: I don't believe in God, so I don't believe in the existence of actual tsadakim. The idea has value, though, for any society, because if you *try* to be one of the righteous people who hold the world together, that's all we can expect from ourselves."

Derrick mulled over the idea, remaining reflexively skeptical. Indulging in the possibility of his own righteousness flew in the face of a lot of his worldview. He would be a terrible member of the Justice League, even if he had the power to absorb the neuroses of the entire League. "You don't think people don't already see themselves as righteous? Especially the irrational ones? Religious freaks seem to have truckloads of that belief."

"That's an interesting question," Phillip admitted, "one that I've struggled with. Every man believes that he is a good person, after all, especially selfish and stupid men. I think that, in the case of overly religious people, most of their righteousness is driven by ego gratification, though; they just want to be seen as having the answers."

"It seems like calling yourself a righteous person is an act of ego gratification, too, though."

"I didn't say that I *was* a righteous person," Phillip countered, "I said I'm *trying to be* a righteous person. It's the same as the difference between being Christian and Christ-like. I also don't think most people feel a responsibility to be righteous and I don't think they're interested in keeping the world intact. The highly religious, in particular, are most interested in lifting their own group up, even if that means pushing others down, and some of a certain stripe are quite literally begging for the end of the world to arrive. In my opinion, that's superstitious and destructive, not righteous."

Derrick leaned forward, planting his elbows on the table and running his fingers through his hair. He needed to get a haircut, but he didn't want his leave his appearance to the mercy of his language skills, so he'd wait until he got back to the U.S. As soon as the plane landed, he'd get a haircut… then figure out where he was going to live for the next year. "Well, sir, you have given me a lot to think about."

"Of course," Phillip said, beaming in between sips. "What else would you expect from a righteous Jew like myself?"

*   *   *

Back at the hotel, still bouncing around from two cups of that shitty, highly concentrated coffee that he drank at Da Vinci's, Derrick flipped on the desk lamp and checked his email. A cryptic message from Shirley lay waiting in his inbox. It simply said, "Call me at my office." In fact, that request served as both the subject line and the entirety of the message.

If it had contained a few exclamation points, an emoticon, or a semicolon wink, he might have felt better about the possibilities… but it also would have confirmed Derrick's suspicion that aliens had abducted Shirley and replaced her with an android. The pessimist in Derrick automatically assumed the worst. Doors in his head started slamming as his brain initiated lockdown mode. Still, once he started inhaling again, there remained a flicker of hope from the part of his mind that had drifted along pleasantly for the last few days, and it insisted that the bad news would be minor. Maybe one of the projects had changed directions but wouldn't be abandoned altogether. Maybe the studio decided to be stingy with handing out screenwriting credits. Maybe the publisher had decided against an advance. He contemplated putting off the call to Shirley for a few hours until he was ready to go to bed, but then he realized that poorly timed bad news might destroy any chance of sleeping that night, Valium or no Valium.

He slapped on his headset, fired up the Skype, and leaned back in the wooden desk chair. Had the chair come with a seat belt, he would have clicked it into place. The phone on the other end rang twice, and

Shirley's assistant picked up and put Derrick through immediately.

"Hey," he said when she answered, trying to sound casual, "what's up?"

Shirley's tar-coated lungs exhaled into the receiver; it sounded like air rushing out of a subway grate. "Are you sitting down?" she asked, her voice grave but not necessarily negative.

He glanced around. "Yeah, I'm on a headset, so I kind of have to sit down to use it," he reminded her. When no immediate reply came, he asked, "Why?"

"The studio dropped the project."

When she said the word "dropped," Derrick felt like his stomach had followed orders and sunk into his feet. "Wow," he said, stunned into numbness despite some dark part of him expecting that exact statement. He stared into the mirror and blinked a few times. His reflection seemed a couple seconds slow. "That was fast."

"Yeah," Shirley glumly explained, "apparently the studio executive who wanted the project changed studios and the guy who replaced him is just running a scorched earth campaign on anything not in production. They do that sometimes with their predecessor's projects, because they basically can't take credit for any successes. Since nothing was signed, we were S.O.L."

"Wow," Derrick said again. He wasn't sure how to react. It felt like climbing out of a wrecked car, where you're taking inventory and hoping that you're not bleeding internally. As long as he didn't start sobbing...

"I know, right?" Shirley said. "No meeting. No re-write. I didn't even get a phone call. They texted me."

"They sent you all that information in a text?"

"Well, they sent the rejection in a text," she explained. "I called over there and found out the rest."

"What studio was it?" he asked, vowing to never watch a movie from said studio or eating at a fast food restaurant engaged in any cross-media promotion with a movie from said studio ever again.

"What difference does that make?" she asked, sympathetically.

"I've found that it helps to focus my hate."

"Hating them is only going to hurt you," Shirley said in a voice that sounded like a sympathetic human's.

"Good point," he said, sighing and letting himself sink further into his flimsy, wooden chair with a creak. Tonight would suck. Good thing he had saved a Morphine tablet for just such an occasion. That little blue pill would swaddle him in a blanket of endorphins and rock him to sleep. "Well, thanks for calling me."

"No problem," Shirley replied, glumly. "Thank god we still have *Re-Ality* all but locked-up. They'll have a contract sent to me in the next couple of days."

"Well, that's good to know." The words left his mouth in a shocked monotone. His voice never contained a lot of inflection in the first place, but this time it must have sounded like a robot calling out from the other end of a tunnel. From the start, he'd fought against accepting the hope this situation offered, but now he realized how poorly he had insulated himself, and the hope was choking him on its way out. *Treat it as a learning experience*, he told himself, reflexively. Next time, he would remember to try harder or try something different to keep from becoming vulnerable... if there was a next time.

"In a way, we're lucky," Shirley went on, now sounding kind of guilty. Derrick certainly didn't feel lucky, but he stayed silent, mildly amused at how she would spin this. "I mean, I hate Hollywood types. On some level, I dreaded the idea of working with those people. You would have hated it."

"Seems like it would have been worth it," Derrick offered, tonelessly. He didn't want her to go away thinking that he didn't feel like shit. Granted, he didn't want to bum Shirley out... she obviously felt bad enough about the situation... but part of her job description involved acting as an emotional fluffer for neurotics. Now, she was going to earn her money.

"I'm so sorry, Derrick," she said, right on cue. "I shouldn't have even told you about this whole situation until I had it in the bag. I was just excited to have some good news for once."

"No, you probably shouldn't have," he told her, automatically, but then added, "but it's okay. You did your best." He couldn't help tossing out that last sentence; it was in his nature... "first, do no harm" and whatnot. He sighed. So much for the fluffing. Maybe he could pay one of the Korean hostesses down the block to say nice things to him in broken English, or at least knock his junk around.

"Well, just in case you're thinking about throwing yourself in front of a subway, remember: once *Re-Ality* gets published, the advance will probably be enough that you can quit temping at those factory jobs for the near future."

"That's good to know." In a weird way, that was probably the highlight of the call for Derrick. Not a lot of people would have made a suicide joke at that time, but Shirley knew him well enough to try. And she was right: all wasn't lost. He just had to load up all of his faith onto the shittiest book he ever wrote...

"And just in case you do it anyway, I contacted your ex about the book rights. She seemed like a real pill, but everything looks good to go on that end." She paused, making a slurping sound as she probably sipped her morning coffee. "Could you explain to me your reason for that one?"

Derrick shook his head. He didn't want to talk about Sylvia, because she would have gotten a real charge out of his most recent failure. He could almost see that barely suppressed smirk and hear the tone of her voice that combined to say, *I can't believe you thought you were anything but a fuck-up.* "Not... right now," he told Shirley. "It's a long story and... I really can't do much talking tonight. I'm going to take some drugs and go to bed. Let me know when things with *Re-Ality* are ready to go."

"I will, and again, I am so—"

He cut her off. Shirley's half-assed platitudes weren't helping. Even if it was too early in the morning for her to bring her A-game, at that point, sympathy grated on Derrick almost as badly as compliments. He started to feel like *he* had let *her* down. The stock phrases continued to roll out of his mouth and into the headset mouthpiece. "Don't worry about it. Have a good night. Day. Have a good day."

He clicked on the red phone icon in the computer screen to end the call, pulled the headset off in the same sloppy manner that broke the last one, and let it fall to the lacquered surface of the shiny wooden desk. Well, shit, he should have expected that. He *did* expect it, on some level, but he should have remained vigilant and... expected it *more*. He tried to remind himself that these things are notoriously unstable. He couldn't remember how many times he'd trawled around IMDB.com and saw that a movie was in pre-production or that a director was attached to the project, and then twelve hours later hearing that production had been suspended indefinitely or that the director was now directing a movie with talking cars instead.

In general, Derrick's life didn't operate in seismic shifts. He designed it that way. Little changes happened, maybe more so with him than for most people, but he didn't live a high-drama life. Sure, he traveled around a lot and worked assorted jobs of more or less importance, but he performed the same routine no matter where he went: work, workout, eat, go to bed, maybe catch a movie once a week. That behavioral sequence provided stability to compensate for the instability of his personality. There weren't many people to create variables in the equation. The last big shift came when he published *Dead Man*, and within the context of his life, that was as big of a game-changer as when homo erectus arrived on the Paleolithic scene.

Under the soft light of the desk lamp, Derrick massaged his numbed face with his hands. His skin felt rubbery, like a mask. This was difficult to absorb. He'd already made little plans in his head about what he would do with the money. He'd buy an apartment in Seattle, that way he'd have a home base and could take his stuff out of storage. He hadn't decided whether to buy one that allowed dogs and cats, because on one hand, he'd wanted a pet for a while, just for that feeling that when you got home, somebody acted glad you were there, but on the other hand, he'd have to find someone to take care of the pet when he traveled. Seattle had a good public transportation system, but he also considered buying one of those completely electric motorcycles that he saw in an article in the airline magazine during his flight to Tokyo. The article claimed that some company was manufacturing a model that was already retailing for under ten grand. Of course, it rained a lot in Seattle...

The fact that all those ambitions had flown out the window didn't constitute a tragedy, not by a long shot, but it helped reinforce the idea that he had peaked as a human, and that the status quo was as good as life would get for him. Literally billions of people in the world had worse lives than Derrick Kessler, but emotions aren't logical, and he knew that if life wasn't going to ever get better, then the current state of affairs was not quite good enough. No one would ever love him until he had enough cash to bribe their affection, and each year, he grew a little older and his annual income shrank a little bit more. Knowing and dreading those facts made each disappointment a little more palpable. He tried to stay in the moment and treat each event with a sense of immediacy, but it didn't always work. Everybody needs *something* to look forward to, even if it's the Rapture.

Thank god *Re-Ality* was getting published.

*   *   *

Chapter Seventeen:

Edna Valenzuela

Shirley sat in front of her home-office computer monitor, staring at the blinking cursor in the upper left corner of the blank, white word processor screen. She didn't see that sight very often... not for very long, anyway. She had files upon files of form-letter templates, and her job largely consisted of opening those templates and filling in the blanks. This time, though, vocation gave way to passion. She would have to create this file from scratch, because art... art simply did not come in template form. Through the power of her imagination, she would transform this immaculate, symmetrical screen into a canvas to receive her masterpiece.

She hadn't attempted to write a novel in five years, but with her firing looming, it seemed like high time to summon her humiliation reserves and take another shot. She never intended to be a literary agent; that was the fallback option that only surged to the fore when the bills started accumulating. When you lose the fallback option, why not take another shot at the dream? She often read journalists' dumbed-down versions of psychological studies in *Psychology Today*, and according to one, a person reaches his or her creative peak in his or her mid-twenties. So, she already had one strike against her... but writing wasn't all unbridled creativity. Knowledge and expertise were necessary ingredients in the artistic stew, not to mention the accumulation of experiences that age provided. Hell, with her contacts in the industry, Shirley stood a much better chance of having a publisher give her book a serious look than she did at twenty-five, even if her ideas would have had a bit more pizzazz back then.

Her battered lungs took as deep an inhale as they could, and her fingertips started dancing across the keyboard. The tension drained from her body, starting at her shoulders and working its way out with each keystroke. She'd been holding onto an idea for about four years for a book based on the summer she spent with her terminally ill aunt, back when she was eleven. The memories of those three months stayed with her all this time, even though she didn't know enough about life to make sense of them until recently. Nearing fifty, she could see that that summer in Ocean City taught her a lot about mortality and about coming to peace with who we are. She never started the book because when she wrote, she needed long, consistent blocks of time; she wasn't the sort of writer who could pick up something a few days after putting it down and re-discover the thread, and her job consisted of a constant string of full of multi-day peaks and valleys of activity.

Also, though, after she started agenting, she didn't want to have to face having her mind-spawn rejected anymore. No one ever *wants* to face that, of course... no one sane... but working in the industry provided some added complications that made it unbearable. The people rejecting her were people she knew personally, not just some faceless names with vague titles. She used a pen name on her submissions, of course (Edna Valenzuela), but just because these editors and publishers didn't know they were rejecting the work of a fellow insider didn't mean that she didn't. They sent her the same stupid rejection letters that went to writing hobbyists. She thought about those letters every time the publishers who rejected her released their yearly list of books, and it never stopped stinging.

More than anything, when she stopped writing, it made it easier to deal with clients. It always made her feel better rejecting a potential client for shitty work when she minimized their pain in her own mind. *It isn't a big deal,* she would tell herself. *So, they can't be a writer. Not all little girls can be ballerinas, and not everybody who takes an Introduction to Creative Writing class can be William Faulkner. You're doing them a favor. They'll get over it and move on and do something more productive with their lives.* She'd taken to calling it her "Simon Cowell Approach," and it worked. It allowed her greater objectivity, but it only worked when she thought of herself as an agent and not a writer. That mantra became a lot harder to recite when only a sliver of difference existed between "them" and you.

Her fingers kept right on dancing across the keys. It felt like a release to type, to create. She especially liked tapping out those first few lines, the automaticity of it. The words seemed to appear on the screen of their own accord. And finishing a book... bringing something into the world fully formed... felt ten times better than starting one. Even if the end product wasn't very good, it came from a place of love, and she now looked forward to that moment of consummation that the coming weeks or months would bring. Maybe after she got fired, she could take a trip down to Maryland and try to find some of the places that she saw when she was visiting her aunt all those years ago, like the boardwalk or that crab shack with the purple exterior that she couldn't remember the name of. Maybe their presence would unearth a few more details, a few more moments of inspiration.

Shirley typed for about twenty minutes, pausing only to write the occasional note on the yellow legal pad to the right of her keyboard or to take a sip from the insulated plastic coffee cup sitting to the left of her keyboard. She could always tell when she was on a role because the sips of coffee became less frequent, colder, and shittier tasting. On a productive day, that sense of satisfaction would make the last drink taste like the best shitty coffee she'd ever drank.

After another twenty minutes that went only slightly less smooth than the first leg, Shirley stopped to read over what she wrote. It looked okay, but…. a little familiar. The child riding in the back of the station wagon, looking out the big back window as someone drove her to a place she'd never been before. The little girl hugging her dog goodbye. It sounded almost identical to the novella she wrote about the girl getting sent to live with a crazy grandfather, except that that one was set during World War II. It never got published, so it wasn't that big of a deal if she did rehash the same idea, but Jesus Christ, she wrote that story fifteen years ago… didn't she have any original ideas left?

She lurched out of the desk before the idea could take hold and marched into the kitchen to reload with the rest of the coffee in the pot. It was too late, though. If her mid-twenties marked her creative peak, she was well on the back side of that now, and the inactivity might have made the trip down steeper. She had to face that fact, not to mention that, while her process skills might have improved from reading hundreds of partially formed manuscripts over the years, but her basic plot and character ideas had atrophied.

Outside, a moving truck splashed its way through a big puddle. Inside, Shirley wondered if she had run out of things to say about life.

She returned to her desk and glumly sipped her coffee, staring at that blinking cursor as it flashed in and out of existence at the end of the word "honeysuckle." The gravity created by the creative cannibalism of her own idea kind of pissed all over her artistic rebirth. *At least I beat Derrick, this time around,* she thought, ruefully. *That lucky little asshole couldn't even think of a title or a plot. All he had was the retarded name: Rick Shaw.* Maybe writing him another email would make her feel better.

*   *   *

CHAPTER EIGHTEEN:
DEAD FLOWERS

"What's your decision, Mr. Shaw?" the man in the pin-striped suit said to Rick, shocking him out of a memory trip, back to a day that he'd spent with his dad, half a lifetime ago. In the memory, the two of them had planned to drive to Lexington for a basketball game, but the water pump went out on the car, and they had to take it to the garage and missed the game. They spent the day walking around downtown, just the two of them, on that unseasonably warm winter day. They got lunch in a diner, and Rick drank a chocolate soda. He must have been ten or twelve at the time, and sodas were a novelty. Then, they walked down the street to the comic store, and his dad bought him The Doom Patrol #42, *one of the few issues he'd been missing. Finally, about an hour before they were supposed to pick up the car, they walked down to the river for no clear reason, other than crisp, cloudless days deserved trees and a river.*

Rick wasn't sure whether the day had remained stuck into his dad's memory cells the way it did for Rick, but it was one of the few days they spent together where spending the day together was the entire point. It was a simple and pure day, and one of the best of Rick's life.

"Are you sure it has to be now?" Rick said to the strange man in the pin-striped suit. They were loitering in the church parking lot under a midday sun that pushed the temperature into the upper eighties. Along with the humidity, the light and heat, combined to make wearing a suit jacket outside a curious choice. Rick's voice quivered, because it, along with the rest of him remained palpably unsettled by all the funeral-related business that had consumed most of his day.

"I'm afraid so," the man said, tonelessly, emotionlessly, obviously trying to strong-arm Rick into making a decision while he wasn't thinking clearly. This dude was the worst sort of stereotype for the financial industry, the sort of man who kept a notch on his desk to commemorate each widow he foreclosed on. "If you aren't willing to take on the responsibilities of an acting president of the company, the board has already decided to go ahead with the merger.

Rick bit his lip. He didn't want to take over the company. He didn't want to move back to Kentucky. He had a life in London that he quite liked... but they had a closed casket at the funeral, and that meant that the last memory he had of his dad's face was the disappointed look from last Christmas, when Rick told him, "Sorry, I can't deal with this right now. I'm sure everything will work out." Things hadn't worked out the way anyone wanted, but every so often, life gives you a second chance. Dad wanted him to be happy, but right now, nothing would have made Rick happier than telling this bloodsucker to shove it.

"Fuck it," Rick said, uncrossing his arms and rising from the bumper of the car. The guy in the suit looked confused, not sure as to what "it" was. "Tell the board they can hold onto their stocks. There's not going to be a fire sale, because I'm taking control of the company."

*   *   *

Derrick spent most of his day shuffling around the city, looking at Buddhist temples. It was a brisk but sunny day, the kind of day where he normally could have walked for miles without breaking a sweat, but the soreness and fatigue from the race slowed him down a little bit. He didn't have much time left in the country, but there simply was a limit to the activities that a person who spoke no Korean could engage in. He already saw the Olympic Stadium when he ran through it at the end of the marathon. The start of the baseball season still lingered a few weeks away. There was probably a bookstore that sold books in English somewhere in a city of ten million, but he could browse bookstores back in the U.S. One positive: at least he could start drinking again since no other marathons lingered on the horizon. He downed two Coronas after finishing his lunch burrito at El Cantina's, the Itaewon Mexican restaurant. A bar sat a few blocks away from the hotel that had a sign in its window indicating that they served Guinness. He planned to head down there at some point, but that would have to wait until the evening, because after the second lunch beer, he felt positively cloyed, like he'd eaten an entire un-sheared sheep. After lunch he decided to walk it off, which led him to the series of temples.

It felt terrible to think it, but the shrines all kind of looked the same. There were bronze statues built in honor people he'd never heard of and geometrically sound, wooden buildings with lanterns to look at, but he doubted anything would stick. He'd forgotten to buy one of those Foder's travel books back before he left New York, so he had to rely on the internet to provide him with the tourist spots worth visiting. He actually ran past several shrines and public squares during the marathon, but of course, he didn't know or care what the hell they were at the time. Various websites provided him with colorful information about the historical localities he visited, which was helpful since he knew virtually nothing about Korean history prior to World War II. He knew that that there was someone of some significance named Nurhaci who died before WW II, but that's mainly because Harrison Ford was trying to bargain away the great man's ashes in exchange for a priceless emerald at the beginning of *Indiana Jones and the Temple of Doom*. Derrick actually took a class in East Asian History, which is the only reason that he knew Nurhaci was a real person. The information from that class, though, like most non-emotional things that happened ten years ago, had mostly faded from memory, swept under by more colorful experiences.

In and of itself, this little, stiff-legged stroll around Seoul didn't provide him with much of a history lesson because most of the plaques were written in Korean... not complaining, but y'know... He popped into an art museum (maybe *the* art museum) for about an hour, but Asian art, to grossly oversimplify, never really appealed to him. Even if French impressionists' paintings hung from the gallery walls, though, it wouldn't have made a difference. He could never endure art museums for more than an hour. At sixty minutes, he reached his saturation point, but after that, since he had already paid the entrance fee, he would usually continue slogging onward, almost as if he were stubbornly trying to get his money's worth. The same thing happened when he went to strip clubs and had to pay a cover charge.

Derrick mainly enjoyed wandering around the city, regardless of whether he absorbed any information from the experience. He had survived the marathon without enduring anything more serious than the typical aches and pains, with the exception of his left knee, which felt like someone had attacked it with a hammer. He always forgot something on long trips; this time, it was a knee brace. At least it wasn't his passport. When he got tired of walking, he bought a coffee, and drank it while reading a few pages of the book he picked up in the JFK airport bookstore about the 1892 Chicago World's Fair. When he had to go to the bathroom, he just dipped down into a subway station to use their public toilets, because unlike New York City, Seoul didn't have to shut down their public restrooms out of fear that homeless people might start living there. He spent most of the day roaming, trying to see what he could see without bothering to understand it. Culture was like that; if you weren't in the know, you never would be. It didn't bother him; he accepted his own ignorance without a struggle.

It also didn't bother him to be the only white guy for a quarter mile in any direction. In America, he always felt detached from people, and here, at least he had an excuse. Here, no one expected anything of him. After being inundated with so many nude Korean men in the gym locker room within a few hours of him walking off the plane, it almost felt like he and Seoul had reached a level of mutual acceptance. Now, he just had to make nice with the rest of the world. Since high school, Derrick had tried to understand the nature of his social failings but, of course, could never quite do it. He appreciated the paradox: expecting himself to figure out his own social deficiency was like asking someone with a blind spot what was obscured by the blind spot. It almost made its own Koan.

The bizarre comfort he felt in his detached strolling through Seoul reminded Derrick of another riddle of his life. He had always wondered if he would feel better about himself (not better overall but better about himself as a person) if he had been horribly disfigured, because then, at least he could blame his personal failings on surface characteristics rather than who he was at his core. From time to time, he was also preoccupied with the idea that he was secretly retarded and that the few modest achievements that dotted his life merely involved people humoring him… like when Carrie White was elected prom queen, except that the ruse was more elaborate. You have thoughts like that when you can't read other people's true motivations to save your life. So, paradoxically, wandering around Seoul made him feel more normal than wandering around, say, Pittsburgh, because there was no expectation of connection.

As he stood at the crosswalk in front of a Lotte fast food joint near downtown, his hands jammed in the pockets of his army jacket as a particularly chilly crosswind enveloped him, Derrick gradually became more philosophical about the movie deal imploding. Yes, it would have been a good thing, financially, if the movie had gotten made, but breaking into Hollywood was never something Derrick had aspired to. He hated fakeness in people, and no matter how many smarmy jackasses you had to deal with in the publishing industry, their numbers grew into legion once you entered the movie world. To put it another way: New York was bad, but L.A. was fucking Mordor.

Everybody says they hate fakeness, even Playboy models list it among their turnoffs, but for Derrick, the fakeness bothered him because of his almost infant-like vulnerability to it. In literary terms, he could read people's manifest content, but not their latent content, so the typical sequence unfolded this way: his inability to read subtext led to him taking messages at face value. This tendency made him look like a chump when people took advantage of him. In response, he kept people at a distance, which made him look like a poorly programmed robot when circumstances forced him into interaction. If fate led him to work extensively with grinning, well-coifed idiots, he might have ended up shoving his thumbs through his eyes.

When he looked up from his thumbs, he found himself standing in front of the window of a relatively unfamiliar Dunkin' Doughnuts ("relatively" because they all had a nearly identical orange and brown interior). Inside, a trio of teenage girls sat at a table, wearing black nylons over their long legs and covering their mouths with both hands while they laughed about some joke completely unrelated to him. The start of his next manuscript (about two, full notebook pages worth) lay in the notebook wedged under his arm, and a mere steaming hot cup of coffee

would unlock that world a second time.   Caffeine and books fit together
so well. They gave Derrick the feeling of control. Life in books was as
simple or complex as you wanted to make it. Protagonists could be truly
honest and forthright, if that's what you wanted. Bad people could be
transparently bad. People could get what they deserved.   ·
If he could, he would live in that world for the rest of his life.

As far as dealing with real people, he always felt lucky that he had
Shirley. Shirley acted as his conduit to the outside world, and even when
she had shifted into Bitch Mode, he knew he could trust her. The few
times, he got sent on book tours and didn't have her as his buffer, and he
didn't know how to act. But you can say awkward, inappropriate things
after you've been successful; it makes you look eccentric. Up until then,
of course, it makes you a weirdo. Would the reverse be true when you
drifted back into obscurity?

*   *   *

Derrick's lower spine sent throbbing pain about a foot in either
direction as he stiffly walked into his hotel room. The stiffness had
gradually crept back into his body, such that everything from his knees to
his shoulders had all but locked up. He immediately positioned himself
with his back facing bed, and with a groan, bent his knees and rolled back
onto the overly firm mattress. Hotel rooms in Korea (and probably most
of East Asia) feature an alcove where you're supposed to remove your
shoes and don plastic slippers for when you're actually treading across the
carpet. Derrick reasoned that it was mostly based on superstition and
tradition, and that it failed to serve any real hygienic purpose (kind of the
converse to dragging your bare testicles across a public couch at the gym),
so he typically stomped around the room in his running shoes just like he
would at a Days Inn in San Antonio. In this instance, he kept them on

when he flopped onto the bed. He might take them off in a few minutes, after his back loosened up, but then again, he might not.

He snatched the remote off the edge of the nightstand and clicked on the TV, but the two stations that featured English-language programming were showing a golf tournament and *Underworld: Unleashed.* Sleeping wasn't an option, because although walking across the city locked up his back, it really didn't tire him out, especially since he finished his last cup of coffee thirty minutes before. So, with no other options, Derrick got up, dragged the computer over to a chair beside the bed, and laid back down and typed with his arms outstretched at an awkward angle. As soon as he saw that Shirley had sent him another email, he swallowed the lump in his throat and wished he'd broken down and watched the rest of *Underworld: Unleashed,* just so he could have forty-five more minutes of contentment in his life. *Long stretches of boredom separated by moments of sheer terror,* he thought, ruefully.

The email, ominously, had no subject line. He clicked on it, and it read:

Derrick:
The publisher dropped the book. I don't know what to tell you, other than that I'm sorry. I'll start sending it out to other publishers again first thing tomorrow. Call me if you want to talk about it, even if it's late.
Shirley

After the first sentence, his eyes crawled over each word individually. Derrick had to remind himself to keep breathing as he read it a second and a third time. He wanted to call Shirley, but he felt more like yelling than talking. Since it was a little past six a.m. in New York, he supposed that, if he insisted on waking someone up, he should at least have something coherent to say. He lay staring dumbly at the computer screen for anywhere between thirty seconds and five minutes. During that point, he read the message one more time, just in case he was hallucinating the first three times. *Nope. Same message.* A few seconds passed before he read it again, just in case he missed a "not" or a "might" that would change the meaning of the message, but it read the same as ever. After a few more seconds of hopeless staring, he decided that he didn't give a shit if he woke Shirley.

With his sore spine now a peripheral concern, Derrick hauled the computer back over to the desk, fixed the plastic headset in place, and punched Shirley's phone number into the computer, but the cyber wormhole routed his call straight to her voicemail without even the suspense of a digital ring. *Of course,* he thought. Agents aren't doctors. The only people who call you before nine a.m. are disgruntled clients and credit card companies. So, just because he had her cell number (one of them, anyway), that phone probably stayed off after six p.m. and didn't turn on again until the next morning.

He grabbed his jacket from the bed and the key from the wall slot before heading out the door. The least he could do was pound down a few drinks before his talk with Shirley and develop some kind of monologue about what he was mad about. He stomped his way through the hotels revolving front door, where a stiff wind slapped the shit out of him. He could barely hear the Korean woman loitering around the car turn-in area say said, "Hey, American. You looking for girls. I find you girls." She was remarkably fat (for a Korean), and she reached out to grab his elbow before he turned and shot her a glare that made her hand jerk away as though he were electrified. He refocused on the path to the bar and marched on.

For once in his life, Derrick actually didn't need help finding girls. The internet informed him that a section of Itaewon colloquially named "Hooker Hill" sat about two blocks away, so unless the name was ironic and it was actually the location of a convent, he could probably find girls there who, for a couple hundred bucks, would treat him like the most fascinating person on earth for a solid hour. He actually considered dropping by that part of town on his way back from the bar, after he got good and tanked and open to bad ideas, then remembered that his projected income for the coming year had dropped precipitously since he finished his race.

*   *   *

He stalked down the street in a hunched position, like someone fending off the cold, except that his army jacket and his anger prevented the chill of the evening from affecting him. He could have emailed Phillip and arranged a meeting so that he could bitch about his life for an hour, but he didn't want to inflict himself on someone who had shown so much generosity to him up to this point. Besides, would someone who grew up in Cameroon really feel genuine sympathy at Derrick's middle-class white man "plight"? *Oh, you can't do exactly what you want for the rest of your life? How dreadful for you! Why don't you stroll on up to Hooker Hill and meet some women who suck dick for money?* And that's a valid perspective, but logic has little to do with emotion. Besides, we all can't be Buddhist monks and have our desires satisfied by a robe and a begging bowl. Derrick charged down the three blocks to the place that sold Guinness (it turned out to be a second-story bar called "The Barrow Boys") and asked the bar tender for one, then sat their hoping that the guy wouldn't pour it like a Pepsi.

As Derrick planted his forearms on the bar railing and stewed, the bartender poured his stout and waited for it to settle before topping it off. A soccer game from some place in the world where it was mid-day

played on the TV. With time to contemplate, Derrick realized that he
wasn't sure who he was mad at. The publisher, of course... not for the
rejection part, that was their business, but for the stringing-him-along
part. A bunch of bush league bullshit. He was mad at Shirley for
presenting circumstances as set-in-stone when they were (apparently)
anything but. He just wanted people to be straight with him. Was that
too much to ask? Just don't fucking lie.

Even with both of those targets accounted for, Derrick had more
than enough anger left over for himself. Why couldn't he have written a
better book? He got his shot at living his dream, which is more than a lot
of people get. The book almost made it across the finish line. If he had
just done *something* different... gone through one more draft, taken out
that stupid metaphor in Chapter One about climbing the rope in gym
class... it might have made it all the way. Did he have to write it in the
first-person? Did he have to set it in a decade (the seventies) that he had
no firsthand experience with? Did he have to make the hero a chronic
masturbator? No, no, and no, and any one of those changes might have
saved the fucking thing from the trash heap.

"Hey, buddy, you doing okay?" the bartender asked. Standing
behind the bar, holding a pint of Guinness with a perfect, one-inch head,
the young man looked like an Irish angel. He wore a blue mechanic's
shirt with grey pinstripes that read "Carl" on its name plate. Derrick
would have bet ten dollars that the guy's name wasn't Carl. It was one of
those names, like "Hugh" or "Lester," that people just didn't name their
kids anymore.

"Hmm," Derrick said, as he lifted the glass and took a long sip
that contained just the right amount of foam. In about two seconds, life
suddenly became manageable, so he forced the deep scowl clinging to his
face to recede. A normal, well-adjusted person would have said that

everything was fine and, gee, that's an awesome mechanic's shirt, and he or she would have said it in a manner that made it come out as natural as the rain. Since Derrick was an abnormal, maladjusted person, he asked this perfect stranger, "Doesn't it feel like God's fucking you in the ass sometimes?"

The bartender had a slightly receding hairline and a bushy fu manchu mustache, as though the latter was going to compensate for the former. Thankfully, he was also youngish, probably a couple years younger than Derrick. In Derrick's experience, older people tended to have problems with (1) public swearing and (2) obscene references to God, especially since George Carlin died, and Derrick didn't want to receive a stern lecturing at this point, and he *definitely* didn't want to get thrown out of the bar before he finished his beer. He was in no mood to drink a plastic bottle of Hite alone in his hotel room.

"Definitely," the bartender told him without hesitation. "You're talking about when you feel like you can't control anything?"

"I guess," Derrick said, then specified. "I'm talking about how you think something is in the bag and you get defeat snatched from the jaws of victory... not to mix metaphors." Talking and (strangely) drinking helped the anger drain away, making way for the influx of melancholy.

"I felt exactly that way with a girl that was here a couple nights ago," the bartender confessed.

"Exactly," Derrick echoed. He allowed that there might be some categorical similarity between their plights, even if they differed by magnitude.

"Is that your deal? Woman troubles?"

"Eh," Derrick considered Shirley for a moment, but he always thought of her kind of asexually, like a chain-smoking aunt. An image of the 21-year-old version of Sylvia flickered through his head, but not as much emotion resonated behind those memories anymore. He remembered that he used to love her, but it almost felt like memorizing a line. She was in the process of spawning a family. If she were a Hall & Oates song, she'd be *She's Gone*. "Not exactly. It's a work thing."

"What kind of work do you do?" the bartender asked, absently wiping out a freshly washed beer glass with a still-white bar hanky.

Derrick normally told people that he worked in a factory, but if he said that this time, it would probably lead to a question about why he was in Korea and what the nature of his problem was, and that would just lead to a web of lies. The bartender seemed strangely intrigued. Maybe because, with only five other people in the bar and two of them playing darts, there wasn't a hell of a lot else to do. At the other end of the bar, a sloppy drunk Korean with a bad comb-over was trying to communicate with a whippet-thin guy who looked to be a member of the American military wearing casual attire. They both used a lot of hand gestures, but it didn't seem to help much in getting their points across. At the back of the bar, another guy who also wore the haircut of an enlisted military man was trying to pick up on the more attractive of the two white girls throwing darts.

"I'm a writer," Derrick said after a few seconds. The words sounded kind of strange coming out of his mouth. He always hated saying it, because it could mean several things. If you define "writer" as someone who voluntarily writes or types words, then John Updike, Jenna Bush, and someone who scrawls dirty limericks on cocktail napkins are all writers. The term really doesn't encompass the sacrifice, or much else about the experience. Most people don't know shit about writing, except what they see in movies (which makes it seem a thousand times easier and

more romantic than it actually is). No one reads anymore, much less
writes.

"That's cool," the bartender said. It came out more like a *good for
you* statement than a comment on the coolness of his writing. It seemed
genuine in the sense that he wasn't blowing smoke up Derrick's ass, but
then again, Derrick had a hard time detecting mockery. "Are you writing
a book about Korea?"

"Not really. I'm kind of blocked up right now," Derrick
explained. He didn't like that he used the term *blocked up*, because it
sounded like constipation, but that's really what it was: verbal
constipation, and it was every bit as uncomfortable as the regular kind....
okay, maybe not *every* bit, but it was existentially unpleasant. "It sucks,
because I thought I had a breakthrough, but that fell through, and now
I'm back to where I was, which is in a financially precarious position. So,
I feel like the next one has to be... perfect."

"Hm," the bartender said, mainly because some kind of response
was required. He obviously wasn't bursting with sympathy. Why should
he? He was tending a three-quarters empty bar in fucking Seoul. "Well, I
think that's impressive you can do that for a living. I tried to do
something like that after I got back from Afghanistan... I know, just what
we need: another memoir about being a soldier in a foreign land... but if
you can believe it, I just didn't have the self-discipline to do it day after
day. When I had other people depending on me, I was locked-in like a
fucking machine, but when it was just me..." He shrugged and absently
ran a damp rag over the shiny surface of the bar as he thought back to the
book that never was. Derrick hoped they wasn't using the same rag he
used to wipe out the glasses. That shrug really said it all, though: why
bother? What purpose does it serve unless you're able to get something
out of it? He stopped wiping and looked up. "Can I offer you a little

advice from someone who's never written anything longer than fifteen pages?"

"Sure," Derrick said trying not to smirk. He'd take advice from anybody this side of a palm reader, right now, but weren't bartenders supposed to be *passive* repositories of your mental anguish?

The bartender picked up the rag. "Did you ever play baseball?"

"Sure. Until I was out of Junior High."

"Never press," the bartender said. "It doesn't work for anything that takes skill. Even homerun hitters can't *try* to hit homes runs. You just have to wait for a good pitch and swing through the ball. Swing hard. Make contact. You *may* hit a home run, but if you're pressing, you definitely won't." He chucked the dirty rag into a bucket and pulled a dry white towel out from under the bar and casually flipped it over his shoulder in a way that indicated that he liked this part of his job. "And that's my advice."

Derrick nodded. "I appreciate it," he said, and genuinely meant it. Part of him wanted to deny that the ten seconds of advice explained his problem, which was sort of true, because it didn't explain the totality of his monolithic Problem. It didn't explain the evaporation of two huge victories. It didn't explain his personality problems. It did mostly explain the writer's block, though, and that was just enough to take the edge off the shitty, stupid day. *Bartenders… is there anything they don't know?*

As he sat, silently drinking the second half of his beer, absently watching the tiny figures drift across the soccer field, he thought about the nature of advice, and how it seldom involved telling us anything we haven't heard before. *Don't press. Take one problem at a time. Focus on the possible.* Clichés, one and all, but useful clichés. Maybe good advice was mostly just someone knowing the right time to remind us of something we already knew but had lost sight of in the storm of emotion.

* * *

"I saw you called earlier," Shirley said the instant she picked up, rather than saying *hello*. At least she sounded fully alert and even-tempered. This couldn't be easy for her; getting the rejection put her ass in a sling, too.

"How did you know it was me?" Derrick asked.

"When you call on the computer, it always comes up on the Caller ID as 'number unavailable.' Combine that with the circumstances and that you called at six in the morning..."

"I see," Derrick said and waited through a couple long seconds of silence. Even half drunk, he wasn't the confrontational sort. And what was he *confronting* her about, anyway? Not being able to sell his shitty book with the retarded title? As soon as he finished a book, he always felt good about it, and it usually took him about a month to form a rational opinion. When the endorphins faded a couple days after he finished *Re-Ality*, he didn't feel good about it at all. He wrote a colorless lead female character, and the plot took two or three painfully unrealistic twists. In fact, when he finally believed that Shirley told him she'd sold that piece of shit, he became almost giddy, because if she could sell that, she could sell anything. Finally, he leaned forward on the desk, head in hand, and asked, "So what happened?"

"Apparently, the person I talked to was one of the editors, and they were still waiting on the publisher to read it. That happens, sometimes; every place has its own procedure. In total, it made it through two readers and an editor, and everybody was high on it, but the publisher thought it was too derivative."

Derrick looked up, only to find his distraught reflection. "Derivative?" he said in disbelief. "It was a lot of things. It was meandering and it was disconnected, but it wasn't fucking derivative."

"You know how these people are," Shirley said, quickly, "there's nothing objective about it. Sometimes they just don't like it deep down in their guts for some undetermined reason and make up something just so they have something to say. They could reject *Flowers for Algernon* for not having enough flowers in it if they wanted to."

"Jesus Christ," Derrick muttered. "This is just… totally fucking back-breaking." He stared at his reflection in the mirror that seemed to have aged ten years since that morning. Maybe it was the lighting… or the booze. "I'm going to have to look for more temp jobs as soon as I get back."

"And with the economy the way it is, you're going to have a tough time doing that," Shirley chimed in, sympathetically.

"True," Derrick agreed, glumly.

"Is there anything I can do?"

"Well, for one, don't taunt me with good news if it's not actually good news," he said, automatically. His reflection gave a thin, humorless smile at that quip.

"I'm sorry," she said. "I normally try to keep my clients well-informed. I know you guys go so long without a lot of positive feedback." Shirley chuckled mirthlessly. "I don't know how you guys do it; if I hadn't quit writing when I did, I'd probably either be dead or in an institution." A pregnant pause hung on the line. Outside the hotel window, a car gave a long, annoying honk. The car horn: the most popular invention in all of Korea. "Don't get too down on yourself; it's still a good book."

"It's shit," Derrick said. "We both know that."

"No, really," she said. "I like all the stuff you write. I think you have a unique perspective on life, and that's the most important thing. You'll get the appreciation you deserve eventually, even if you end of being one of those people whose work isn't appreciated in his own lifetime."

"Oh, thanks for that," he said. "Can't wait for the glowing reviews in the *Obituaries* section. At least I can look forward to having my burial paid for, right?"

"I meant that as a compliment," Shirley chided, as gently as she was capable. "Some people are just ahead of the cultural curve, and I think you're one of those people. I know you didn't start writing just for the money, so it should make you feel a little better knowing that people are going to enjoy your work, eventually."

"It doesn't," he assured her.

"Well, at least you'd be helping someone out. I guess your ex-girlfriend in this case," Shirley said. He pictured Sylvia reacting to the news of his death, maybe on the local news. She'd probably show more emotion if the cable went out. "I'm sorry I got morbid, but that's an unfortunate reality of art: some people aren't appreciated in their own time, and it usually takes some sort of human tragedy for people to stop and finally take time to notice the work."

"I guess," Derrick said, absently, suddenly not feeling very chatty. "I better go. It's late here. I think I might try to check out of the hotel a little early and see if I can get some of my money back. A little of it, anyway. Thanks for talking."

"No problem."

"No, really. I mean it," he insisted. "I don't say it enough, but I really appreciate what you're *trying* to do for me. I just wish I could give you something better to… work with."

This time she paused, maybe to see if he was finished. "No problem," she said again. "Have a good night."

*   *   *

CHAPTER NINETEEN:
KILLING ROVER

The call ended, and Shirley set her cell phone down on the top of her office desk and removed the ear buds that supposedly reduced her chances of developing brain cancer. Despite the reassurances, after stressful phone calls, she thought she could feel a massive tumor forming behind her eye sockets. *Well, congratulations*, she thought, absently scratching the back of her hand. *You always wanted to inspire people, and now you're inspiring one to throw himself in front of a bullet train.* She couldn't even comprehend what a train traveling 200 miles per hour would do to a human body. *Even if he manages to keep from killing himself, you've made him hate himself and feel utterly worthless... more so than usual... and it isn't even ten a.m.* Now, her elaborate plan required that she sit back and hope her well-timed lies had their intended effect.

The only sounds in her office came from the rush of the air vent and the melodic sound of Kenny's eerily mistake-free typing next door. Kenny had a real talent for that. In a different world, maybe he could have been a concert pianist (assuming he could read music). Instead, he

was working for her... for now. How did some people manage to endure
life without a sense of humor?

She took another sip of her morning coffee, and it actually made
her feel a little more lively. Nothing tasted better than the first coffee of
the morning, unless it was a submarine sandwich after a hangover. She
stared up at the vent, unable to tell whether it was exuding heat or air
conditioning. It was one of those sixty-plus-degree, tweener days.
Somehow, she now found it a little harder to hate Derrick than she did
two weeks ago. He was just so... pathetic. Not in a totally worthless way,
but in a totally helpless way. She could tell him George Lucas was
standing in her office and wanted him to star in a remake of *Star Wars*,
and, at least in his mind, he'd start working on his light saber fighting. He
wasn't stupid, but when it came to interacting with real-life people instead
of words on a page, he behaved like a high functioning autistic: he
couldn't tell when someone liked him, when they were joking... or when
they were lying to him and trying to get him to off himself. That's
probably why he kept people at such a distance, because when he let them
in, he was totally incapable of defending himself.

One thing was abundantly clear: Derrick trusted her... which
made the task of deceiving him about as challenging and enjoyable as
coaxing the family dog to jump in the car so you could drive him to the
vet's office to get euthanized. Maybe she'd have felt better about the
direction things were going if she were getting a bigger payoff for all the
pain she inflicted, like if he'd signed his book rights over to her instead of
his insanely unlikable ex-girlfriend. Maybe. That certainly would've been
nice, because in the coming days and weeks, she was going to need all the
steady income she could get. His decision to fork over the book rights to
his ex never came as a shock, though; emotional people are so
unpredictable.

An unread manuscript sat on the edge of her desk. Shirley decided to take a bathroom break, top off her coffee cup in the shared kitchen, and go through the motions of working her job while she still had it. Fifteen years and zero job security. At least she had her sense of humor.

*   *   *

Chapter Twenty:

Unnervingly Numb

Derrick clicked on the red, downward-facing phone icon on his computer screen to end the call. Several minutes passed before he worked up the motivation to remove the headset, and several more minutes passed before he so much as shifted in his desk chair. Normally, the wooden chair pressed into his back at an awkward angle felt terribly uncomfortable, even for hotel furniture, but his entire body had become so numb that he might as well have been sitting in a beanbag chair. All the anger had deserted him, and he couldn't think clearly enough to remember the name of the next Kübler-Ross phase. On a typical night, he would try to knock out a couple pages before going to bed (and then delete them in the morning), but he wasn't sure he possessed the wherewithal to successfully stand up and walk to the bathroom. He glanced around for a plastic bottle with a wide mouth, just in case.

Strangely, as he sat slumped in the chair, staring at the slightly sagging skin of his aged visage in the mirror, he thought about Sylvia… but that thought soon faded in favor of a consideration of all the benefits of jumping in front of a subway train. One obvious benefit was that he wouldn't have to endure that awful flight to O'Hare from Seoul. He'd have to break into a hospital pharmacy to make it through a flight that long and depressing... and that's if he *got* an aisle seat.

He couldn't get past the idea that his life really hadn't amounted to much, and there was no indication that it ever would. He hadn't inflicted any irrevocable damage on anyone, but that kind of constituted a negative accomplishment, something he could have managed even if his mother had miscarried. He once wrote a book that a few people enjoyed... then he treaded water for a decade. Fate gave him a chance, but he couldn't do anything with it.

When there is nothing tethering you to the ground, it's so easy just to disappear. He could vanish into thin air and escape the stench of his own failure, and it wouldn't make a damn bit of difference to anyone. At best, he didn't dislike his life so much as find it... utterly pointless, and he saw it continuing on in a similar vein, except that he would get older and slower, and the decent, normal people of the world would find him more and more bizarre. If he offed himself and, by punctuating the oddity of his life, that act helped him sell books, at least he'd be able to have accomplished *something* meaningful because he could give the few resources he'd accumulated to someone who had built something, who wasn't just going to piss it away.

The image of Sylvia with her faceless husband and genderless kid flickered in his head again. He had been in love with Sylvia once, and while she did turn out to be a bitch and a fraud, there was no denying that she had made him happier than anyone ever had. Alarmingly happy, in retrospect. Stupid-happy. And while that also made him vulnerable, he'd certainly never approached that level of happiness since. Shouldn't there be some kind of reward for that? He never turned out to be the writer or the man he wanted to be, but a little bit of steady money certainly would help her out. He'd never have any kids, but he could make a contribution to her kids' futures. It was sort of a legacy. It was better than nothing.

Breaking down the math, he found several reasons to jump in front of a subway train (or better yet, go down to the passenger train station, buy a ticket, and jump in front of one of those KTX bullet trains that go 200 miles per hour… yeah, that would be better, because most of the subways in his area of Seoul had interior Plexiglas barriers that didn't open until the train arrive, no doubt a byproduct of a society with the highest suicide rate in the industrial world). In contrast, he found fascinatingly few reasons not to… other than that it might hurt (which he didn't believe) or that he might go to hell (which he *really* didn't believe). All he really had to lose was his life.

In a moment of inspired focus, Derrick rose from his chair, a horizontal pink line creasing the middle of his back, and moseyed over to his luggage. The fuzzy shock still enveloped him, but it wouldn't last forever, and when it left, it would take the remains of his backbone with it. He reached into his side zipper pocket and retrieved his travel-sized Dramamine tube and unscrewed the top. Most of the contraband he'd brought along was the low- to medium-dosage Hydrocodone. Not enough to kill him, but enough to give him something to look forward to on a daily basis. For emergencies, though, he did bring one tiny tablet of the good stuff: Limbaugh-grade Oxycontin. He shook the pill into his hand. It might as well have had a smiley face drawn on it. Neurologists showed that the same part of the brain activates when we're experiencing pain, regardless of whether it's pain of the emotional or physical variety. Maybe that's why this shit cured the blues so well. Screw antidepressants…

He popped the pill into his mouth and choked it down without the aid of a drink. Hopefully, it would start working before he had to endure the humiliation of crying alone in a foreign land.

*   *   *

CHAPTER TWENTY-ONE:

THE AXE

Shirley stepped into Doug's office, thinking *He's going to fire me.*
The thought practically made her lips move.

"How are you doing, Shirley?" Doug said as she sat down in one
of the cushy office chairs across from his desk. He swiveled around in a
high-backed model, even better than the one Shirley had. This one was
made out of green leather and had pivoting arms and a headrest. Most of
the stuff in his office was either the same shade of green as the chair (e.g.,
the curtains) or starkly white (e.g., the paint on the walls). This color
scheme served to remind visitors that Doug attended Dartmouth.
Otherwise, Doug's office was distinct from the other offices at the agency
for its lack of loose paper.

Shirley sat rigidly in the chair, her linked fingers covering the top
kneecap of her crossed legs. She wore beige slacks, and she desperately
wished that she had ironed them that morning… as if that somehow
would have saved her. "I'm fine," she said aloud, evenly, but internally,
she thought, *He's going to fire me.* Out loud, she added, "And you?"

Doug leaned back in his chair to show off the pit stains of his white, collared shirt that he wore without an undershirt. It wasn't a hot day, but the sweat pattern on his shirt made it look like he ran to work. He scratched his thick mass of greying hair in an aggressive way that always used to make Shirley think he had lice. Now, the scratching just made her think that he was going to fire her. "Not too good," he said, allowing his arms to ease back down and flop onto the armrests. "It's no fun being a boss in a bad economy."

"Probably better than being an employee in a bad economy," she quipped, feeling slightly drunk. An absent smirk stretched across her face when she heard the words come out. *Good one*, she thought. Normally, that comment wouldn't have passed through her social filter, but these were abnormal times, and the social filter may have blown a fuse. She and Doug never got along during the eight hears he'd been running the agency. Part of it came from their vastly different senses of humor: he thought the *Scary Movie* movies were hilarious and she… well, didn't.

They didn't have an especially bad relationship, though, until she made the comment to Emily Silverman about Doug looking like Meat Loaf right as she and Emily stepped out of the Ladies' Room, where they found Dough standing beside the candy machine, eating Milk Duds. The whimsical nature of fate: if he'd bought a Three Musketeers or a Zagnut, or anything that wasn't made from 100% caramel, he probably would have finished his candy and walked on down the hall before she exited the bathroom and finished her poorly timed observation. As it was, he heard her comment in mid-chew, and his jaw froze as their eyes met. Emily's face lit up in mock horror, then she quickly skulked down the hall with her head down. Shirley followed a couple long, awkward seconds later. She and Doug never spoke about the incident. I mean, what can you say?

He looked *exactly* like Meat Loaf without the long hair (i.e., *Fight Club* Meat Loaf, not *Paradise by the Dashboard Light* Meatloaf).

To be fair, Shirley's middling record over the last year put her on the endangered list, but that stray comment made sure that her neck fell on the chopping block as soon as that became an option he could get away with. She knew she was in deepest of deep shit the instant she saw the note from Doug's secretary sitting in her inbox. She didn't even need to read it; it made her go numb just to see that telltale sheet of yellow legal paper folded into thirds.

Doug took Shirley's comment about being an employee in a bad economy in stride, probably wishing he had a few Milk Duds to chew on so that he had time to think of a clever retort or something philosophical to say that would make the decision seem as natural as the tides. "True enough," he finally said, adding a fake little, knowing chuckle. "True enough."

Shirley had never been fired from a job before, and it turned out that she got a little squeamish waiting for the executioner's axe to fall. Doug probably had a whole speech concocted, something that used a metaphor about the agency being a family or a ship full of deckhands or something equally stupid, and she would have paid a thousand dollars not to listen to it. "Doug, am I getting fired?" she asked, making sure to force eye contact.

Doug's eyes widened. "Well, I don't like to think of it in those terms," he said, defensively, almost to the point of sounding hurt. "I mean, there's nothing personal about this."

"Of course not." She allowed the hard "t" to linger. *Maintain eye contact*, she told herself.

"It's a simple fact that we have to let somebody go," he said, absently straightening the pens on his desk while Shirley stared at him with her arms folded across her chest, "and based on the money that's coming in... or not coming in, that would be you, lately.

"*Lately*," she said, "being the operative word." She kept her voice even. "Did it ever occur to you that the person with the most productive clients one year would be at a disadvantage the next?"

"You didn't have the most productive—"

"I was close," Shirley assured him with far more confidence than she actually possessed. It was true that she didn't approach her job with nearly the gusto that she used to, but who did? She wasn't a machine, and she wasn't a sap. Besides, managing the eccentricities of disappointing clients like Derrick had sucked the life out of her. "Look, I don't give a shit. You're paid to be a pragmatist, not to be creative or empathic. Hell, we all are. Just tell me how long I have."

"Well, if you sign this waiver," he said, quickly whipping out a sheet of high-end paper from his desk drawer, "saying you won't poach clients, you can finish out the next two weeks. If not, you have until the end of the day to vacate your office." He meekly pushed the paper, which had sat lurking in the room the entire time, toward her end of the desk.

Shirley stared at the paper as the fear and uncertainty that it represented boiled up inside her. Where would she go? Her track record had sucked lately. Who would hire her in this economy? All security was relative, and absolute security was an illusion, but she'd been immersed in that illusion for many years, and having it pulled away made her feel naked. The feeling didn't last long, though. She exhaled in a long, steady sigh; two weeks wasn't going to matter, either way. "Well, the end of the day it is," she said, slapping both knees and standing up. "It's been a lovely ride, Doug, before and after you got here. I'm going to miss this place."

*   *   *

Shirley eased into her office chair one final time. She paid for the chair herself, almost two years ago, but removing it from the office and storing it in her apartment would cause her more trouble than it was worth. She still might do it out of spite. That's mainly why she kept the threat of poaching clients on the table, just to inconvenience Doug. She wasn't even totally sure she wanted to continue working as a literary agent. Sure, she could probably land another job before her unemployment benefits ran out, sick economy be damned, but seniority would be lost, and pimping out other people's work never made her feel like she ever built anything. You're just a middleman, shepherding the product through the process and taking your cut at the end. Maybe this… firing would allow her to take a little time off to work with children… or scale Mount Everest. Either of those might be rewarding. Granted, she really didn't like children or nature, but at least in the case of children, she could teach them to not act so whiney.

A couple weeks ago, she'd started taking her office home, handfuls at a time, mostly papers. Someone who worked there could have walked into her office and wouldn't have known anything was different, though, because she had only emptied her cabinets and drawers; the visible pillars of paper remained like some sort of modern art Stonehenge. Last week, she brought in two big, collapsible boxes early in the morning and stashed them in her otherwise empty cabinets. As fate should have it, she drove to work the morning of her meeting with Doug. Now, if she could just find Luis or one of the other Dominican janitors who worked in the building, she could pay him ten bucks to carry the boxes to her car. If they took off the wheels, they could probably cram her chair in the back seat of her Altima, too.

Despite an inability to claim any concrete accomplishments (people remember who wrote and published a book, after all, not who haggled for an advance), boxing up the rest of her office did bring back a lot of memories. Old Christmas cards from clients had collected in the bottom of her desk. Despite the fact that she knew her clients were just being business-nice, like when they tipped the mailman, she still had difficulty throwing the cards away. She also found a few forgotten pictures from forgotten book fairs. She looked sober in most of the photos, and the clients smiled those happy smiles and caused their little cherubic faces to flicker back into her memory cells. Even though they were ephemeral, it was the client relationships (make that "the *successful* client relationships") that made the job worthwhile. She got to bask in the presence of people during some of the happiest moments of their lives. When you had something to do with it, when you caused it, you got to sponge off of that drug-like feeling of *triumph*. And if the situation was reversed and she had to deliver bad news… well, then she could always order Kenny to make the call.

Writers were such a sensitive group. Fiction writers, anyway; people who write books about dog grooming and the South Beach Diet aren't exactly investing themselves in their product the same way as people who create an alternate world, populate it with interesting people, then kill off those interesting people in slow, painful ways. Novelists, even the ones who wrote about flesh-eating demons and throat-slitting commandos, invested their dreams and their nightmares into those books, and you had to admire them, even when the final product sucked… hell, decidedly that… *especially* when the final product sucked. Submitting a manuscript was like asking out the prettiest girl in school when you only have a less than one-percent chance of success. In this business, you had to stick your neck out that same way every single fucking time. She knew what taking that risk felt like, and she knew intimately the sucking feeling that came with failure. That was why she felt as much pride as she did about having delivered so many of them through this cruel process.

She peered into her middle desk drawer and picked up her saber-shaped letter-opener. The soft office lighting reflected off the polished metal as she turned it over in her hands. For a brief period around 2005 or 2006, she kept stack of unopened letters on her desk, just in case somebody came in her office to flip her shit, she could wield the knife-like letter-opener in an "unintentionally" menacing way. She sighed and placed it gently in the box. So many memories...

What would happen to Kenny? She never gripped the inevitability of her situation such that she could raise the issue with him, but that didn't mean Doug wouldn't unload Kenny's salary even faster than he did hers. Hopefully, Kenny heard the rumors floating through the halls, just like she did, and had enough time to prepare. Other than typing, he really didn't have any marketable skills... did he? He must have submitted a résumé at some point, but she didn't remember anything remarkable about it. Sure, she could offer to let him go with her to... wherever she landed, but the thing was, he really wasn't—

She jolted upright, causing her chair to squeak. Wait a minute. Didn't she just counsel a client to commit suicide? And if he did, wasn't he still being represented by Doug and the rest of the carnival freaks who worked in the office? Oh, that would not do at all. Her fingertips drummed on top of the desk. She needed to contact Derrick immediately.... Immediately after her final smoke break.

*   *   *

CHAPTER TWENTY-TWO:

REBIRTH

Derrick woke up around six in the morning but lay staring at the ceiling as daylight crept into the room. When he finally climbed out of bed, the clock on the nightstand read "9:10." It took him that long to think of a reason to start the day, and he finally settled on promising himself that he would order a glass of orange juice with his breakfast. He hadn't treated himself to a glass of O.J. in a while, certainly not for breakfast. After that, hopefully he could think of a reason to make it to lunch, but he would cross that bridge when he came to it.

He slouched his way down the sidewalk toward Dunkin' Doughnuts, looking more hung-over than the two disheveled American military personnel he passed on the way. He failed to check his email before leaving the hotel room, and for this violation, the reflexive tug of routine gnawed at his nerves in an obsessive-compulsive kind of way throughout his breakfast. He suppressed the feeling. Part of him hoped that someone might have emailed him regarding a change of heart, but hell, at the rate he was going, another part of him expected his inbox to contain a message that his apartment building had exploded or that he was being sued for plagiarism… or both.

As Derrick sat down in one of the doughnut shop's thinly cushioned chairs with his orange juice, coffee, and muffin, drowning in regret, a funny thing happened: the urge to check his email on schedule had been replaced with a desire to write. An idea for a scene popped into his head, where the main character sits talking with a younger version of himself about the fate of the world. They are sitting in a coffee shop in Korea. He didn't totally know the context the scene took place within, but at least it was an honest-to-god scene, not just the name of a character.

He reached into the pocket of his olive-drab army jacket and felt around. His fingers touched on a bandana, a half-consumed pack of Valium, and a mildewy Avis Rent-A-Car map of Anchorage, Alaska. Ultimately, he removed the white, 8½-by-11 inch papers that listed his hotel and flight information and a black hotel pen, and proceeded to write his way through a large coffee, muffin, ham-and-egg breakfast sandwich, and an orange juice, and it didn't even feel forced. When he absolutely had to go to the bathroom, he hobbled back across the street to the hotel and continued writing while seated on the can. By the time he'd finished, he'd blanketed every white space on the front of and back of his travel papers, along with a healthy chunk of hotel stationary. He guessed that it amounted to about nine pages worth of thought-gasm. No personal productivity record, to be sure, but unlike the ideas for the Rick Shaw book, he didn't immediately hate it the second he stopped writing. Thus, it appeared that he had an idea that would give him a reason to get out of bed for at least one more day, and right now, that was enough.

Between the orange juice, the production, and the cleansing bowel movement, his mood had substantially lightened by the time he plopped down at the desk to read Shirley's most recent email. The subject line was: "Your ex is a bitch. Don't give her your books." That was the content of the message, too, except that she wrote out "ex-girlfriend" instead of abbreviating it.

*   *   *

CHAPTER TWENTY-THREE:

TRUE BELIEVERS

"Does it seem self-indulgent to say that I wish I wasn't so self-aware?"
Young Rick asked the old man as they walked slowly across the arched, stone bridge to
the other side of the gently gurgling brook. To any passersby who bothered to notice,
they undoubtedly looked like father and son… maybe even grandfather and son… out
for a Sunday stroll. The resemblance was almost too perfect, like when a police artist
tries to age someone from a photograph. The hair had thinned in the right spots, and
there was a stoop to the old man's walk, but every feature and movement stayed
comfortably within the same ballpark.

"Of course it does," Old Rick said," because they're two sides of the same
coin. You can't achieve self-awareness unless you ponder over your own motivations.
And you can't ponder over your own motivations without lapsing into self-indulgence
from time to time. The key is this: just accept it, or else you're going to make the
situation worse. Everybody's got something about their personality that stands out.
You're self-indulgent. You aren't a psychopath, you don't have religious delusions, but
you are self-indulgent. Just accept it and move on."

Young Rick watched the water from the rushing stream churn below. It was a windy day, but the temperature must have hovered in the upper fifties, which was where he liked it: too cold to sweat, but not cold enough to cause the stinging pain that came with winter. "I guess," he said, automatically. It's what he said when he needed time to digest things. Old Rick knew this, of course.

"That also means you have to accept your self-awareness, and what comes with it," Old Rick explained. Young Rick had to delay his leg swing about half-a-second and shorten his stride to allow Old Rick to keep up as they walked. "What did Spider-Man teach us?"

Young Rick strained to search for the trick to the question, but couldn't find one. "With great power comes great responsibility?" he offered.

"Exactly."

Young Rick smirked, he liked verbal pats on the head, and he was self-aware enough to know this. "So, what's my great power?" he asked with just a hint of cheek, although he probably should have said "our great power."

Old Rick gave the question a couple seconds to linger in the air, but when he finally spoke, he still didn't answer the question. "I like to think about the super-heroes," he said as he shuffled along, the bridge turning into a paved bike trail leading deeper into the park. Between the blue sky, the clear water, and the classic autumn foliage, it was a strikingly beautiful day, more reminiscent of Central Park than Kyoto, but Old Rick seemed to focus on keeping his feet moving forward more than anything. "Saying something like that sounds childish, for some reason, but they inspire me to think beyond the likely. Most of them had super-human powers, but they were just things normal people could do, but just to a greater degree. Some people are fast, but not as fast as The Flash. Some people are strong, but not as strong as The Hulk." He paused to gather himself. The combination of the speech and the walking was sucking the air out of him. "Batman was always considered oddball; the super-hero without a super-power. People think of him as a holdover from the days of the pulp detective comics, like The Shadow or The Green Hornet, and that he didn't quite fit in with the modern age of the earth-bound gods… but that's because most people think about the physical… the quantifiable. Batman's super-power was his willpower. He had the willpower to mold himself from a child kneeling in his parents' blood in the streets into the pinnacle of human perfection."

Young Rick felt a weight building in his chest, and he didn't like the sensation. He felt more breathless than the middle-aged Japanese guy in running shorts who just jogged past them in stiff, choppy strides. Maybe it was all the talk about what would happen to the environment over the next fifty years. Maybe he and Old Rick were body-swapping, like in that awful George Burns movie. "What does that have that have to do with —"

"We know ourselves," Old Rick explained, already knowing the question because he asked it once, half a lifetime ago. "We know ourselves well enough to know when we're being selfish and when we're being stupid and when we're being emotional. Since we know these things, we can stay objective when it comes to considering the likely consequences of our actions. This gives us the power to act because it's the right thing to do, not because it feels good at the time."

Young Rick glanced up at the sun peeking through the foliage as he took another deep breath of autumn air. It felt cold and dry, and he wondered if he'd been holding his breath. "That doesn't sound very pleasant. Like having all the disadvantages of being a robot without any of the advantages."

"It isn't very pleasant," Old Rick said with a distant, long-toothed smile as he looked out at a fragile world. "There are many days when you'll want to disappear into the bliss of ignorance. But when times get tough… and they will get tough… just remember your Spider-Man."

*   *   *

Shirley closed the cover of the book, and the assembled group of thirty or so Barnes & Noble customers clapped politely. "Thank you all so much for coming out tonight," she said into the microphone when the clapping died down. She used her most congenial voice, the one she typically reserved for decision-makers she met for the first time. "To tell the truth, this bookstore has always had a special place in my heart. I worked in mid-town for a lot of years, but I would always make the extra trip down here to Union Square whenever I would have to do any personal shopping. So, thanks for making my first appearance as a... public figure so terrific." Another smattering of applause. Polite, but genuine, which was good, because if they clapped too lustily, she would assume they were related to her. "I've been told we have some time for me to take questions from the audience."

A twenty-ish Indian woman (curry, not casino) sitting in the front row held up her hand. She looked bright-eyed and eager, and maybe because Shirley admired her sparkle, she called her instead of the white-haired guy in the back who looked like a lit professor. The girl stood up, a bit self-conscious about speaking in front of nearly three dozen people. "Hi, thanks," the girl said. "I was a fan of Derrick Kessler's work since *Dead Man in Sheets*, and listening to you read from his last book really makes me wish I'd been old enough to listen to him at a reading."

"Honey," Shirley said, smiling and rolling her eyes for effect, "I practically had to put a gun to his head to get him to come to these things." The crowd laughed, politely, but the laughter petered out when they people in the audience matched the implication with the most prevalent rumor about Derrick's fate. Shirley did that from time to time, and whenever someone called her out on it, she acted like it was an accident, but in truth, she liked to remind them.

"Yeah, um," the Indian woman continued, awkwardly, "I was just wondering how it felt to get his last manuscript after his disappearance. I mean, was it like getting a message from... beyond the grave?"

"Well, he sent it from South Korea, which isn't quite the grave," Shirley said, and waited for the modest laughter from the audience

members who had visited Korea... or at least wanted to pretend that they
had, "but I'd just gotten unceremoniously fired from my job at the
Douglas Graves Rights Agency after having worked there fifteen years...
even before Doug Graves ran it." She also liked to throw that fact into
public statements whenever she could so that it could paint Doug as the
ungrateful bastard that he was. "So, it took almost a month and a half for
the manuscript to find me, but saying that it was a 'message from beyond
the grave' makes it sound like something creepy. I suppose you could say
it was a little like that it was like the last goodbye from an old friend you
thought you'd never see again." That got a few sympathetic head tilts so
she poured it on.

"I happened to be home when the package arrived, and when the
mailman handed it to me, I didn't immediately know it was from Derrick
because the return address had gotten mangled at some point on its trip
from East Asia to New York, but his awful handwriting was a little
familiar since he never figured out how to print labels and hand-wrote
everything. So, I tore open the package and... I can still remember
reading one word at a time: '*Tsadakim* by Derrick Kessler.' Well, it was
like I'd been hit by a freight train."

Another murmur from the crowd at another of her *accidentally*
tasteless comments. Shirley ignored it and called on a youngish man with
a patchy beard and a yarmulke pined to the back of his skull. "Uh, yeah,"
he began, "I was wondering, what exactly was your contribution to the
story?"

"Well, I did all the editing and wrote the last couple chapters,"
Shirley lied and let a smile play across her lips as her eyes took on a distant
look. "Derrick always liked to hold the last couple chapter back and make
me guess the ending." It was yet another lie, but it got another round of
head-tilts, which was all that mattered. Acting. She should have gone

into acting. Maybe she would have, but when she was an undergrad, you had to spend your first year fucking around in set design. Too late now...

"Well," the young man said, a little indignantly, "one of you misquoted several sections of Hebrew texts, you realize?"

"You're right," Shirley agreed, nodding, then shifted her eyes past him. "Next question?"

*   *   *

It was a cool autumn night, and Shirley needed a smoke, so she decided to walk a couple subway stops over before letting the train take her the rest of the way home. A ringing emanated from the depths of her woolen coat after she'd finished her cigarette and stood under the red glow of a KFC sign, about half a block from her intended subway station. She reached into her coat pocket and fished out the phone. Her display screen said "unknown number," but she knew that it was an international call... from Marseille, France, to be exact. She answered the call. "Isn't it, like, two a.m. there?" A long pause as she strolled half a block to the stoplight. "Yeah, if you think *that* boosted sales, wait until your miraculous resurrection." Another pause. "You don't have to be so generous; I'm having the time of my life. Besides, even if you are a tortured artist, you're still the best client I've ever had."

THE END

www.ingramcontent.com/pod-product-compliance
Lightning Source LLC
Chambersburg PA
CBHW032001240626
47153CB00003B/1077